"Braydon, I'm only going to tell you this once. I don't, and will not, blame you for the actions of a psychotic man. You did *nothing* wrong."

"But now I'm afraid he's after you." She may not have known Braydon long but she did know that the vulnerability he was showing now was rare. It pulled at her heartstrings.

"We don't know that for certain," she said.

"He wants to make me suffer. What better way than to use you."

"You care about this entire town and all of its people. He can use any of us." She said it to lighten the mood. They were skating around saying something significant again. Sophia could feel it. She watched as the conflicted man next to her chose his words carefully.

"He knows you're different."

MANHUNT

———

TYLER ANNE SNELL

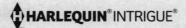

This book is for my mother, Robin. Who, against all odds,
has never stopped believing that I can do no wrong. Without
her support and never-faltering love, this book might still be
a tangled web caught in my head. I love you, Ma!

Recycling programs
for this product may
not exist in your area.

ISBN-13: 978-0-373-69829-5

Manhunt

Copyright © 2015 by Tyler Anne Snell

Printed in U.S.A.

www.Harlequin.com

Tyler Anne Snell genuinely loves all genres of the written word. However, she's realized that she loves books filled with sexual tension and mysteries a little more than the rest. Her stories have a good dose of both. Tyler lives in Florida with her same-named husband and their mini "lions." When she isn't reading or writing, she's playing video games and working on her blog, *Almost There*. To follow her shenanigans, visit tylerannesnell.com.

Books by Tyler Ann Snell

HARLEQUIN INTRIGUE

Manhunt

CAST OF CHARACTERS

Sophia Hardwick—Finally on the right track to a successful career, this city girl has to drop everything when she learns her older sister has gone missing. Now she's in the small town of Culpepper, Florida, trying to piece together a dangerous story to save the only family she believes she has left. Can this self-made woman help solve the case while keeping her distance from the detective with aquamarine eyes?

Braydon Thatcher—Eleven years have passed since the incident that changed his life forever. The newly appointed detective now vows to bring justice to those who deserve it. But when a new case stirs up the past, can he make good on his promise to save those in trouble? Can he finally find the peace he's always wanted in the form of a certain beautiful, stubborn woman?

Lisa Hardwick—Older sister to Sophia, Lisa's life is seemingly perfect before she vanishes without a trace. Was she taken, or did she have a reason to leave?

Amanda Alcaster—One of the three women to go missing after a blowout fight with her mother, she leaves behind more questions than answers.

Trixie Martin—With no apparent ties to Lisa or Amanda, this social recluse is reported missing, further complicating the case.

Richard Vega—Lisa's boyfriend and the last person to see her before she disappeared, the wealthiest and most liked man in Culpepper isn't a stranger to secrets. Is he really trying to find her, or did he have a hand in her disappearance?

Cara Whitfield—Knowing what it's like to be an outsider, this Culpepper beat cop forms a quick bond with Sophia as well as a personal determination to find the person responsible for the disappearances.

Tom Langdon—Braydon's partner and closest friend, this easygoing detective is one of the few people who know the truth about Braydon's tragic past.

Chapter One

Detective Braydon Thatcher looked at the dock with an anger he had learned to contain burning in his chest. No matter the time that passed, that spot was his personal hell.

"I just don't understand! Amanda and I fight sometimes, but nothing so bad that she'd just leave."

Braydon tore his eyes away from the dock, no longer in the Bartlebee name but that of the Alcasters, and took in the rumpled Marina Alcaster. She was upwards of sixty but looked as frail as if she were pushing eighty. Her slumped frame and thin bones were deceiving at best. Everyone in Culpepper knew she had a temper that often boiled over and ran hotter than the Florida heat. Her screech could be heard like a car crash in the town square.

Which was why no one, not Braydon or his partner Tom Langdon, was surprised to hear that Amanda had gone. Though, her mama refused to entertain such a thought.

"When's the last time you two had it out?" Tom asked, sending Braydon a significant look when Marina hesitated. "Did y'all fight last night?"

Marina pursed her lips and shifted a hip out. "I wouldn't call it a fight...but we did have a conversation."

"A conversation?" Braydon raised his eyebrow as Tom wrote that one down. "What kind of conversation?"

Marina put a hand on her hip. "A loud one." She huffed.

"Was Amanda mad when this loud conversation ended?" Another hesitant look.

"Well, yeah. She got in her car and left." Before Braydon or Tom could point out that Marina had called to file a missing-persons report, she rushed on. "But she came back later! Look—" she pointed over her shoulder at a blue Honda "—that's her car!"

"And you haven't seen her since?"

"No, that's why I called you two." Marina's temper was starting to flare and Braydon didn't have the patience to deal with it today. Not with the dock looming in the distance with its invisible stain of agony. Tom, one of the only constant friends Braydon had kept since the incident eleven years ago, knew his partner was distracted by the closeness of it. He took down Marina's contact information and assured her they'd look into it.

"We'll give you a call when we find her," he called, already following Braydon to the truck. "I bet you thought after your promotion to detective you'd have a lot more interesting cases than dealing with a little Alcaster dispute, huh?"

Tom was trying to lighten the mood Braydon had fallen into—he smiled big, exposing teeth slightly stained by too much coffee. Braydon appreciated the gesture and shook himself as they pulled out of the driveway and took the winding dirt path back to the main road.

Tom was right, though. Braydon expected—and hoped—for more exciting work than looking for Amanda, who was twenty-six years old and probably at a friend's house waiting for her own anger to sizzle out. Not to mention, her being gone wasn't an actual case until she had been missing for forty-eight hours. The only reason they had driven out was due to a lull in between cases. Also, it wasn't wise to anger the elder Alcaster, which is exactly what would happen if they had told her to wait her daughter out. So out they had come, ready to help a member of the community. Though, again, trying to patch up a fight between mother and daughter hadn't been on Braydon's mind when he signed up for law enforcement. For the better part of his career, he had worked hard for the promotion to one of the two detectives in Culpepper. The town wasn't big by any means, and mostly sleepy, but there were still investigations that needed working and cases that needed solving.

Plus, it wasn't the promise of excitement that had pushed him into the profession—it was the pursuit of justice.

"Have you ever met Amanda?" Tom asked, facing ahead so the sun lit up his blond hair.

Braydon nodded. "I've been to a few parties with her but that was when we were in school," he answered. "I had to be about seventeen…maybe eighteen." That had been almost eleven years ago, Braydon calculated. Back when he was going through the wild and rebellious stages of being a teenager—drinking, partying and feeding hormonal impulses at every turn. He had been one of the undesirables then, on the wrong side of the law that he now tried to uphold. His mother had sent him to church every Sunday as if it would absolve whatever demon had possessed him, but there was nothing Pastor Smith could preach that would end Braydon's lust for the wicked.

That is, until one rainy night changed everything.

Tom seemed to realize the bad mood was relapsing. He shifted in his seat and turned up the radio. The cool sounds of 103.1's program of all things '80s pumped through the truck's speakers. Normalcy returned in the small cab.

The end of September had crept up on the town, though the Culpepper heat still radiated like it was August. Sweat pooled beneath Braydon's white polo shirt, adhering it against his suntanned skin. One of the perks of his promotion—shedding the uniform. Despite his reformed sensibilities, wearing the cop getup pricked against his inner rebel.

It was a twenty-minute trek from the Alcasters' back to the station at the heart of town. Braydon spent the rest of the drive watching the rural part of Culpepper transform into neighborhood turnoffs, industrial buildings, shopping boutiques and the few dilapidated structures littered in between.

This part of town had once been run-down—a meeting place for drug dealers, prostitutes and people who liked and used both. It wasn't until six years ago that Richard Vega had pumped life, and money, back into the four-block stretch. The New York City native had a business acumen to be reckoned with and enough funds to open Vega Consulting—a company of marketing strategists created to serve not only Culpepper, but all of North America.

Braydon didn't know the extent of how Vega Consulting operated, but he had to believe they were doing well. Richard Vega lived at the end of Loop Road with an electronic gate surrounding the five acres of land he had purchased without batting an eye.

The partners had fallen back into a comfortable silence the last few minutes of the drive. It was as though the growing distance from the dock was lifting a sour weight from Braydon's shoulders. When the police station came into view, the ill feelings had all but disappeared, though Braydon knew he wouldn't get any sleep tonight.

"Langdon," Tom answered after his phone did a vibrating dance.

Braydon pulled into the parking lot that butted up against the side of the station. The building dated back to the '50s and had been renovated at least three times. It was all brick, cracked tile and offices that were small enough to pull double duty as closets. When most officers, Tom included, complained about the state of the building, Braydon found he didn't share their sentiments. He never felt more at home than when he set his eyes on the place.

He turned off the truck and met the humidity with a deep breath. It was midmorning, and the heat was at its worst. The rain that had bathed the town hours earlier had done little to reduce the temperature. He smiled to himself. There wasn't a cloud in the sky. Despite all of the opportunities he'd had to leave his hometown, it was beautiful days when the sun was shining that reaffirmed his decision to stay. A person just couldn't beat a beautiful day in Florida.

"Okay, we're right outside now." Tom hung up the phone and followed Braydon around the building to the front double doors with Culpepper Police Department hung in rusting letters above them.

"There's a woman waiting in your office," he said, holding the door open. "And apparently she's not too happy."

Braydon quickly ran through the list of women he had been with in the past few years, trying to find a name that stuck to someone who might be pissed. Well, recently pissed. Angela had been the last woman he had been with but that had been two months ago. Surely, she wasn't the one in his office pitching a fit.

"She's from out of town," Tom offered, cutting off Braydon's line of thought. "Probably got a ticket from John and wants to complain to someone." John was a policeman who loved giving tickets to tourists passing through. Some people loved golf, John loved giving tickets. Braydon sighed.

"I'll deal with her," he said, feeling his nerves switch to annoyed. He'd never had much of a stomach for outsiders.

"Sounds good to me. I'm going to call around and see if I can't find Miss Alcaster."

They parted ways after walking through the lobby and into the largest room in the station. Rows of desks, computers, chairs and coffee cups filled the room. Some were occupied with Uniforms—a few colleagues Braydon didn't like and a few who didn't like him. John the Ticketer's chair was empty. He was probably writing someone up right now, Braydon mused. Along the far side of the room stood four doors that led to a break room, Tom's office, Braydon's office and the conference room. To the left, with the blinds always shut over the window in the door, was Captain Westin's domain.

A man was smart to avoid that office when the captain's temper was high.

Braydon walked across the room and let out a sigh as he saw his door was closed. Why they had left a stranger unsupervised was an issue he would bring up as soon as he ushered her out. Not only was it an invasion of privacy but also breaking regulation.

He reached out to grab the doorknob when the old oak slab flung open.

"It's about damn time!"

Braydon stepped back, caught off guard. He furrowed his brow at the woman standing before him. No one in Culpepper would believe she was anything but an outsider. Despite the heat and humidity, she was wrapped in a black pantsuit with a blazer that covered the length of her arms and a shirt that dipped low in a V. Although Braydon tried to keep his gaze up, he couldn't help noticing the suit hugged her chest and hips in a very attractive way. Her skin was creamy porcelain, another sign that Florida was not her home. It stood out like a shock against the glossy dark hair that was pulled high in a bun. Although her eyes were a deep shade of sage, there was no denying the fire that sparked behind them.

"I've been waiting in here for almost half an hour!" she fumed.

Braydon put up his hands. "Whoa, calm down. Why don't you take a seat and we'll get this all straightened out." He moved around her, catching a whiff of perfume. It filled his senses with its sweet aroma.

The woman hesitated, as if unable to immediately obey, before she dropped down into the seat across from his desk.

"Now, Mrs...."

She waved her hand through the air. "Miss," she corrected impatiently. "Sophia Hardwick." The name sounded vaguely familiar but Braydon couldn't quite place it. The red-lipped Sophia had scrambled his attention. "And like I told the man out there, I'm here about my sister." She was gearing up to explain, her hands intertwining on the top of the desk. The way she leaned forward a fraction, didn't improve the hold on his concentration.

Before she could start, Tom appeared in the door. His brow was furrowed. He didn't bother with knocking.

"Braydon, we need to talk." He tipped his head toward Sophia. "This will only take a minute, ma'am."

Sophia slammed her hands onto the desk. She stood with such speed that Braydon mimicked the act, hand flitting to his holster.

"Are you serious? You just got in here. I've only had time to tell you my name for heaven's sake! You will not put me off anymore," she said, looking between the men. "I'm here because my sister is missing and I need you idiots to do something about it." There was a pause as all of the air seemed to rush out of her. Color tinted her cheekbones, whether from the exertion or her makeup, Braydon didn't know.

"I didn't know Amanda had a sister," he said, lowering his hand but still on guard. Sophia may have been petite but her passion was seeping out of every pore.

"What? Who's Amanda?" she huffed. "I'm here about Lisa." Braydon looked at Tom, who had turned white as a sheet. Something must have happened as soon as Tom had gone to his office.

He looked down at a paper in his hands. "Lisa? Does she happen to go by Trixie?"

Sophia shook her head. A few strands of hair came loose at the movement. Tom's upbeat mood was gone—an issue that brought Braydon's nerves back to the edge.

"No. She goes by Lisa. Lisa Hardwick."

Tom's mouth set in a deep frown. Without explanation to Sophia he turned to Braydon. "We need to talk," he said. "Now."

"Unbelievable! I just tell you that my sister is missing and you just—"

"Ma'am. We will be with you in a second," Tom snapped. It was a rare occurrence to hear the shorter of the two men so tightly strung that Braydon didn't hesitate. He followed Tom into the conference room two doors over.

"What was that about?"

Braydon didn't know what answer to expect but it sure wasn't what came next.

"Cal Green, you know him?"

Braydon nodded. "The mechanic?"

"Yeah, well he left a message a few minutes ago. He says his secretary, Trixie Martin, hasn't shown up to work for two days. He got worried because she wasn't answering her phone and headed to her place. All the lights were on, the TV, too, and the front door was unlocked. He talked to the nearest neighbor but they didn't see or hear anything. Her car was even in the driveway." He didn't wait for Braydon to respond. "If that woman in your office is telling the truth, then that means—"

Braydon felt like he was waking up—all of his senses stood alert.

"That means that we have three missing women."

SOPHIA WAS FED UP with all of the interruptions Culpepper had to offer. From the moment she had stepped foot inside the police station it had been a stream of one after the other—keeping her from asking whole questions, let alone getting full answers.

She had been bounced from officer to officer only to be told to keep quiet and wait for the lead detective to come in from a call. So, there she had stayed, sans the quiet. The four-hour trip had strung out her already thin patience as she left voice mail after voice mail on Lisa's phone. It wasn't her fault that the Culpepper PD wasn't prepared for her volley of loud complaints.

Sophia smoothed out the invisible wrinkles in her slacks and tried to keep her temper in check as the minutes ticked by and the detective hadn't returned. On a normal day she would have been more understanding, perhaps more patient. She knew that if she were back home in the city, the chances of her still waiting in the department's lobby would be great. At least here she had been ushered into an office. Small blessings and silver linings.

Being alone was something Sophia had grown accustomed to throughout the past few years, but she found the lack of communication now was grinding into her anxiety. Lisa might fly by the seat of her pants 80 percent of the time, but she had never been so irresponsible as to leave without saying a word. Their relationship may have become strained lately, but it wasn't that strained.

"Sorry to step out like that." Detective Thatcher walked back into the office with a notebook under his arm. Instead of sitting behind the desk, he leaned on its corner and tilted his head down to meet her gaze. His eyes were the color of the sea—swirls of aquamarine. They were the kind of eyes that captured a person, making them want nothing more than to get lost within the bright pools. Sophia hadn't noticed their allure until he was so close.

He had a swimmer's build—tall, lean, but with muscles that peeked through his clothes. His shirt was pulled taut over broad shoulders, while his sun-kissed skin was a rich bronze—a shade she hadn't been able to achieve in the muck of Atlanta. In contrast to his partner's thinning blond hair, Thatcher had a mass of dark brown locks that were mussed to mimic what she thought would be his bed hair.

Sophia realized she had been staring. She needed to pull it together for Lisa. She cleared her throat and pushed her back straight.

"Now, if you would start from the beginning," he prompted. His long, and ringless, fingers wrapped around the pen. He wrote with controlled precision as she spoke.

"My birthday was four days ago, on Sunday," Sophia started.

"Happy belated birthday, then."

She waved her hand dismissively but said thanks. Turning twenty-six hadn't felt any different than turning twenty-five. "Lisa was supposed to come celebrate and she didn't. And before you come up with a bunch of excuses as to why she didn't show, let me stop you. My sister is an intelligent woman who, despite her occasional bout of forgetfulness, is one of the most responsible women I know. I've been trying to get a hold of her since yesterday. I called her cell phone, her house and even her work."

"Have you been to her residence?" Thatcher asked, his eyes piercing. Sophia shifted, suddenly uncomfortable.

"Yes, she obviously wasn't there."

"Was there any kind of disturbance? Did it look like someone had been there recently?"

"No, but that doesn't really surprise me. From what I've heard she practically lives with her boyfriend." Thatcher raised an eyebrow, this quiet gesture asking more than any verbal question would. "She isn't at his place, either. He's the one who called me yesterday asking where she was."

"Wait, didn't you say she missed your birthday was four days ago? Why did you wait until yesterday to try to contact her?"

"We haven't really been on the best of terms this past year." Sophia's face heated. "I assumed she didn't come because she didn't want to. It wasn't until Richard called that we realized she had been missing for two full days already."

"And Richard is the boyfriend?"

She nodded. "Richard Vega, I think he owns a company in town."

Thatcher's expression sharpened, his brow furrowing together as he paused writing.

"Your sister is dating Richard Vega? As in Richard Vega of Vega Consulting?"

Sophia nodded, more hair fell away from the bun atop her head. Whatever Thatcher was thinking, it wasn't showing in his expression. His calm demeanor had turned utterly blank.

"And why didn't he file a missing persons?"

Sophia felt her eyes widen. "You mean he didn't?"

Thatcher stood and beckoned his partner from the other room.

"Did Richard Vega file a missing report a few days ago?" The blond man didn't leave to go check. He instantly said no.

"We would have heard if Vega came here."

Thatcher scratched his chin. It was smooth—void of facial hair that would hide the perfection that outlined his face. How kissable it looked, Sophia would have thought, had anger, fear and suspicion not been vying for the top emotional spot. Richard had called her with a voice drenched in worry. When she admitted she had no idea where Lisa was, he had assured her he would have it taken care of—that he would take all of the necessary steps to find her sister. Sophia had assumed that meant talking to the police.

"Why wouldn't he have talked to you?" she asked.

"That's a good question," Thatcher said before leveling his gaze. There was a look she couldn't decipher behind the eyes of the detective. All she knew was that it comforted and scared her at the same time. "That's a very good question."

Chapter Two

Detective Thatcher's cool expression returned as he ordered Sophia to stay in his office. He sent in one of the beat cops, Officer Whitfield, to take down an official statement with all of the contact information between her sister and her. Whether he sent in a woman thinking it would make her more cooperative, she didn't know.

Cara, as she was told to call the woman, was curt but kind and even though her gender didn't affect Sophia's mood, she managed to dot all the i's and cross all the t's.

"Don't worry too much," Cara said with a smile that contrasted her darker skin. "Detective Thatcher is one dedicated man. He'll locate your sister and bring her back, no problem." She went as far as to pat Sophia's knee. "I'm sure she's just lost track of time or is staying with a friend."

Sophia resisted the urge to disagree and instead pasted on a smile. Maybe the woman had softened her attitude a bit, but that was only patching one spot in a dam that was ready to burst. If she didn't get some answers soon, there would be no man or woman in the whole town who could keep her from exploding.

"Thank you for waiting," Detective Thatcher greeted when he came back in. He nodded to Officer Whitfield as she collected her things and exited.

"Well, I seem to be doing that a lot here."

Thatcher ignored the pointed response and leveled his gaze at her.

"Miss Hardwick, do you know any women by the names of Trixie Martin or Amanda Alcaster?"

Sophia didn't have to think about that long. She shook her head. "No."

"Those names don't ring a bell at all? Maybe your sister, Lisa, has mentioned them?"

She crossed her arms across her chest. "No, I don't recall her talking about them. As I stated before, Lisa and I haven't been on the best of terms recently. There's a chance she may know them, but I couldn't help you with that," she answered honestly. "What does that have to do with Lisa being missing? Do you think they took her?" She compiled a quick list of why someone would kidnap Lisa. For one, she was beautiful—long legs, big bust, thick black, tangle-free hair and a pair of lips that drew men's attentions from a mile away. Lisa was also annoyingly perfect when it came to socializing. She knew how to command a room and entertain an audience. She also seemed to be dating a man who carried a lot of weight in town. Surely any or all of those reasons could make a few women jealous.

Detective Thatcher scratched at his chin, staring through her as he thought. When he realized she needed an answer, he straightened.

"I don't think so." His answer was made to put her at ease, but it wasn't as concrete as she would have liked.

"Then why are we talking about them and not about Richard and the fact that he *did not* report my sister missing?"

"I'm about to go question him myself," Thatcher said, pushing off the desk. He handed her a piece of paper.

"That's my office number and my cell number along with Detective Langdon's numbers."

Sophia raised her eyebrow. "And you're giving this to me why?" It was his turn to look confused.

"So you can contact us if you hear from Lisa or think of anything else that could help this investigation."

"But you just said you're going to go talk to Richard, right?"

"Yes, I certainly am."

"I'm coming with you, then." Sophia stood and pushed her bag up her shoulder. Detective Thatcher looked less than pleased but she didn't care. She had up and left her job as an office manager at Jones Office Supply, traveled from the big city to a town that in comparison would barely fit in a shoe box, all while being submerged in a pool of worry. She didn't want answers—she needed them.

"We'd like it if you would stay here and answer a few questions to help us, Miss Hardwick. Don't worry, I'll ask Richard all of the important questions."

"I can answer questions later, *Detective*. Right now I want to go see what Richard has to say." She crossed her arms over her chest. She was glad she hadn't changed her outfit since work that morning. The heels gave her the height to feel intimidating.

Thatcher mirrored her stance, crossing his arms over his chest. The biceps that flexed at the movement didn't lie about his workout habits.

"Listen, you've made it pretty clear that you don't know much about your sister's boyfriend or this town, so let me enlighten you on a few things." He made sure she was focusing on what he said next. "Richard Vega is the wealthiest man in Culpepper. He is also one of the most loved residents. Pissing him off and yelling at him won't get you any answers. At least, no truthful ones. If you want to come with me you need to calm down and try to keep a level head. Got it?"

Sophia nodded, slightly offended. It was true that she wasn't the best with confrontation but why Richard didn't report Lisa missing was a big question she was more than capable of asking. Unless Thatcher was arresting her for something, there was no way he could stop her regardless. She knew how to work the GPS on her phone—she could get to Richard's by herself. Sophia would go over the detective's head or behind his back if necessary. He must have guessed as much. After a tense moment he let out a long sigh.

"You're riding with me, then," he said, not trying to hide his annoyance.

"I have my own car, thank you."

"Listen, if you want to come along, you're riding with me."

"Why?" she asked, voice raised. Was this some kind of cop-civilian power trip? She wasn't afraid to start yelling again.

"Because I want to make sure you come back to answer those questions." He took his keys out of his desk and motioned for her to go through the door. "I have a feeling you aren't a person who respects any kind of rules."

Sophia tried not to blush as she struggled to get into the cab of the detective's truck. Her heels, now more cumbersome than intimidating, snagged on the small step up making her look like a drunken fool as she stumbled inside. At least Thatcher kept his mouth shut and pretended not to notice. If she had been Lisa, the movement would have been effortless and graceful.

"How far is it to Richard's?" Sophia asked as they turned out of the station's parking lot.

"You've never been there?" he asked.

"No, I haven't." She shifted uncomfortably in her seat, guilt starting to move through her stomach. "I've never met the man, either."

"And how long have Richard and your sister been dating?"

Sophia rolled her eyes. "Over a year now." She set her jaw and mentally dared him to ask why she hadn't met him. He must have picked up on her body language—he shut his mouth and they rode in silence until he finally answered her.

"Richard Vega lives on Loop Road. We have about ten more minutes until we get there. He lives on a large piece of land so it's farther from the town center."

She nodded. The anger she had felt toward the detective was lessening as she struggled to bat down her aversion to his authority.

"I do follow the rules, by the way," she said after a few minutes had passed. "I just—" She looked down at her hands. "Lisa is the only family I have left. Well, the only one who counts at least. So, I've been kind of high-strung lately." She felt her cheeks heat up again as she tried to apologize for her rude behavior without actually having to say it.

The detective glanced over before he sighed for the second time that day.

"It's okay. Situations like these are stressful." He hesitated before continuing. "We were late into the station because we were on a call about a woman named Amanda Alcaster who was reported missing. There's also another woman, named Trixie Martin, who was reported missing within minutes of us arriving."

Sophia sucked in a breath. She didn't know what to process first.

"I wanted to tell you so when I bring it up to Vega, you don't freak out," he continued. "This all could just be a misunderstanding or some women who want to escape their lives for a little while. But on the off chance that it isn't, I need to make sure I approach the only suspect we have with caution."

"I'll keep quiet, then," she said after a moment. "But I still want to be in the room."

"Deal."

IF THE DETECTIVE hadn't told Sophia that Richard was the wealthiest man in town, she would have known the moment she saw his house—if it could even be classified as something as typical as a house. It sat at the end of a small one-lane road and could only be accessed by being buzzed in at a gate just outside the large loop driveway. The more Sophia looked at the place, the more she wanted to classify it as a mansion. It was only two stories but it expanded wide on both sides, looking like an old plantation home. An expansive garage sat to the left of the main house and beautiful, meticulously groomed landscaping was placed in between as a testament to some gardener's handsomely paid green thumb. Large white columns lined the front porch a few feet from the driveway while the double, red, arched front doors were held open by someone who looked suspiciously like a butler.

"Who's that?" Sophia asked as Thatcher opened her door and helped her out. Normally, she wouldn't have accepted his help but she didn't want another awkward moment in front of such an impressive abode.

"I never remember his name, but that's Vega's assistant. He's a mousy fella, but you can't see Vega without getting through him." Sophia let Thatcher lead the way to the well-dressed man. She wondered if his boss bought him the suit that he wore despite the humidity which played havoc with her hair.

"Detective Thatcher," the man greeted, shaking his hand. He looked over his shoulder to Sophia. Recognition flared behind his mud-colored eyes. "Miss Hardwick, it's nice to finally meet you." On reflex she shook his hand.

"I'm sorry, but do I know you?"

The man laughed and shook his head. "No, but Lisa loves to show us pictures." Sophia had to roll her eyes again. That certainly sounded like Lisa.

"Mr. Vega is finishing up a meeting with some vendors. He shouldn't be long." He led them through the front door and immediately to a large open room to the left. Sophia was almost disappointed she couldn't take a tour of the house. Just from the front door she had seen a large, marble-white staircase with a banister worthy of being a makeshift slide. "Make yourselves at home. He'll be in here shortly." The assistant scurried off, shutting the door behind him.

They were obviously in what was used as a formal study. Built-ins lined the walls from floor to ceiling and were filled with matching sets of thick-spined books. A large, formidable desk faced the door, no doubt to keep an eye on those who might enter, while high windows were draped in translucent cloth. A rug the size of Sophia's living room cushioned the noise of her heels on the hardwood. She walked around the room, wondering if Lisa spent any time in it reading.

"I knew Richard had money, but I didn't realize how much," she admitted to the detective. He kept still in the middle of the room, looking as out of place as she felt. His jeans and plain shirt were a few leagues below the apparent dress code that Vega's staff employed on a regular basis.

"They say he works hard," Thatcher replied.

"They?"

"Like I said, this town loves Richard Vega." Sophia wanted to ask what *his* thoughts on the man were, when the door opened.

Richard Vega was all suit, hair product and posture. He walked into the room as if it had been his idea. As if *he* had been the one to invite Detective Thatcher into his home. Watching him make his way over, Sophia immediately understood why Lisa was so drawn to the man.

There was an undeniable overriding sense of confidence that rolled off of him in waves. Lisa had always been drawn to, not just strong, but powerful men. She had a track record of getting involved with the big dogs only to realize what they had in confidence they lacked in kindness. Lisa had assured Sophia that this man was different, that Richard Vega had a good heart, but now Sophia didn't know if she bought that assessment.

Although he was handsome—tall, blond and tanned, angled facial features—Sophia found herself thinking that the detective had him beat. A thought that made the color rise in her cheeks. She glanced at Thatcher from the corner of her eye. He was straight-backed and concentrated on the approaching man. She doubted he was thinking about how she might be more attractive than Officer Whitfield or any of the other women in the station.

"Detective," Richard said, extending his hand. Thatcher shook it, though there was a stiffness to it. "And you must be Sophia. Your pictures don't do you justice." They shook hands. "I'm sorry we had to meet under these circumstances."

"Yes, let's talk about those circumstances."

"Of course, let's sit." Richard was at least smart enough to know that sitting behind his desk while the two of them sat in chairs on the other side was not the best move. If this had been a business meeting, he would have been the man in charge, but this was an investigation and Detective Thatcher was the one calling the shots. Richard instead situated himself on one of two leather love seats at the far side of the room.

Sophia and Thatcher took the one opposite, the small furniture making their legs touch. She made a point not to look at him as he leaned forward, slipping into detective mode. She also tried to ignore how her heart sped up at his closeness. At the station she had been at the man's throat but now he was pulling at her concentration. She didn't need distractions right now. Lisa couldn't afford it.

"Let's jump right into this," Thatcher started. "You called Sophia Hardwick on Tuesday morning around six-thirty asking for the whereabouts of her sister, the woman you've been dating for over a year. Correct?"

"Correct."

"When she told you she didn't know, you told her you would take care of the situation. Again, is this correct?" Richard nodded. At each question his jawline tensed. "Sophia says that her sister never made it to see her. You found this out, so that puts Lisa Hardwick unaccounted for since Sunday morning. That's four days, not even including today, that Lisa has been missing." Slowly, Richard nodded. "So tell me, Mr. Vega, why the hell you didn't call us or file a missing-persons report?" There was no mistaking the anger in Thatcher's voice—nor the hidden accusation beneath his question. Having the whole situation recounted had a similar effect on Sophia. She wished she had as much experience as the detective at spotting a lie or pressing on a weak point to get the right information. Instead she kept her mouth shut and decided to follow whatever lead the man next to her would take.

Richard kept his face calm, not at all surprised at the question or its parallel series of thoughts. He leaned forward, elbows on his knees, and looked between them.

"I had a potential client come in Saturday night. It was a last-minute announcement but I wanted to show this person that I could be flexible and that I was very interested in taking on his business. If he agreed to work with me, then I could get him to participate in or donate to the Culpepper Fund-raiser this year."

"The what?" Sophia had to ask.

"It's a fund-raiser scheduled for next week. I started hosting them a year after I moved here. The town buys tickets while various organizations hold different auctions to raise money. It's also a banquet of sorts—champagne, food and music."

Sophia's eyes widened as she remembered where she had heard about that before.

"That's where Lisa met you."

"Yes, the first one she came to she picked it apart, saying the vendors had ripped me off and that she could do it better if she was in charge." He smiled. "I thought she was joking but Details did a great job last year."

It was Detective Thatcher's turn to raise his eyebrow. "Details? Why does that sound familiar?"

"It's an event-planning business Lisa started when she first moved to Culpepper," Sophia responded. It was also one of the reasons that they had drifted from each other.

"Got it. Now continue, Mr. Vega."

"Lisa helped me host a very small, informal gathering here in the house with said potential client and a few of my employees."

"And does this potential client have a name?" Thatcher asked with a raised eyebrow.

"I'd like to keep that confidential, if you don't mind. We don't want any rumors going around before anything is official."

"I do mind," the detective said with seriousness. "But we can get back to that later." Richard didn't miss a beat as he continued.

"We stayed up well into the next day. However, Lisa turned in early and left early. I, on the other hand, ashamedly slept in until almost noon. She had left me a note saying she was heading to the birthday party and would call when she made it. I turned my mind back to the potential client's entertainment needs as well as business and before I realized it, it was Monday." He balled up his fist. "I didn't question the fact that she never called until Monday night after my guest left. I called her and got her voice mail." He switched his gaze, now intense, to Sophia. When he spoke his anger was palpable. "I assumed you would have called if she hadn't shown up. I just thought the silence was the two of you doing some sisterly bonding thing and Lisa just forgot to call. Why didn't you call when she didn't show up?"

Sophia's face flushed red—a mix of embarrassment, guilt and anger.

"Lisa and I haven't been on the best of terms this past year," Sophia almost spat, trying to defend herself. "You should have known that. She didn't tell me she was coming, so when she didn't show up *I* assumed it was on purpose."

There was a heated silence, not at all like the thoughtful one she seemed to share with the detective when they were sorting through new information. This was weighted. This was bogged down with ill feelings and regret.

"Continue, Mr. Vega," Thatcher said, commanding the two of them to snap out of it. Richard looked back at the detective and let out a loud breath.

"When I still hadn't received any word by Tuesday morning, I decided it wasn't just Lisa's forgetfulness. The phone call with Miss Hardwick here just confirmed it. I left work and began looking for her, only to come up empty."

"Why didn't you call us?"

Richard sat up straighter. "At first I thought…" He paused, trying to find the right words. "I thought that Lisa had left me, using Sophia's party as an excuse to disappear."

"Why would she leave you?"

"Over the past year, I've grown to trust Lisa more than I've ever trusted anyone else. She has become not only a woman I care about, but a confidante." At this admission, Richard for the first time seemed uncomfortable with what he was saying.

"She knows secrets about you," Thatcher said.

"Not only personal, but professional. Secrets my competitors would pay big for. Secrets that could undo everything I've worked for my entire life. I've had much worse attempted by people who want my money or business before."

"Lisa wouldn't do that, though." Sophia spoke up with certainty. "From what I know, she has been very happy with you." Richard's intense expression softened at that.

"I couldn't rule it out entirely. So I called in a few favors and had her phone traced." He didn't bother acting sheepish. "I found it."

He shared a look with Detective Thatcher. It sent a chill through Sophia.

"And?" she prodded.

Richard stood and went to retrieve a box under his desk. He presented it to Thatcher. The contents made Thatcher's brow furrow. Sophia was almost afraid to look but she had to be strong. She had to be strong for Lisa.

Holding her breath she peeked in.

"Is that it?"

Richard nodded, frowning deeply while Thatcher pushed around the several pieces of what once was a cell phone. Sophia felt her stomach drop.

"Before it was smashed, I was able to follow it to the main road, just past Tipsy's Gas & Grill." Sophia looked at Thatcher questioningly.

"It's a family-owned gas station and mini-restaurant off of the main road," Thatcher explained. "Busiest gas station in town." He motioned to Richard to continue.

"When I went to where it last was turned on I found it scattered along the side of the road." He sent another significant look to Thatcher.

"I'm assuming you already tried to salvage the SIM card inside? To recover any pictures or—"

"None of it could be saved." Richard dropped back into his seat. "I couldn't even find the remnants of the card."

"So, what does that mean?" Sophia asked.

"It means," Richard began, running a hand through his hair, "that either Lisa doesn't want anyone to find her or someone doesn't want us to find Lisa."

THE AIR SEEMED to zip out of the room—leaving behind an unsettling silence. Braydon felt Sophia tense next to him. It was a response he was familiar with when bad news was flitting around.

"Did you find anything else?" Braydon asked. He

wanted to know if Richard was aware of the other missing women.

"I called the hospitals and even morgues in the neighboring cities looking for her or a Jane Doe who matched her description, but nothing came up." He pulled out a card and handed it to Braydon. "I even hired two PIs from this firm to search the cities."

"You hired out-of-town private investigators before you contacted your local PD?" Braydon said incredulously.

"I hired them to stay *out* of town to find her. Culpepper is small. I had faith, if she was here, that I'd run into her."

Braydon was fighting the urge to yell at the very rich, very pompous man in front of him. If he had just called the police when he first realized Lisa was missing, it could have made all the difference, but instead he wanted to handle it himself. He had as much pride as he did wealth.

"You still should have filed a report," Sophia barked out, breaking her silence. "Did you ever think 'What if she didn't run away?'" Braydon could tell her composure was cracking.

"Of course I did. I'm not an idiot."

"Well, you could have fooled me!" Under different circumstances, Braydon would have smiled at Sophia's brashness. She didn't bottle up her emotions—she let them pour out instead. The two of them would have kept on, but Braydon had had enough.

"Do you know Trixie Martin or Amanda Alcaster?" Braydon watched the man's facial expression closely. He could see wheels turning but there was no concrete recognition of either name.

"Not personally. The Alcaster name sounds familiar, but what has that got to do with Lisa?"

Braydon took a breath. Sophia's hands fidgeted across her lap. He wanted to hold them still, to keep her worries at bay. Personal experience had taught him that as long as a loved one was out there in trouble, no one, not even he, could quell all worries. That didn't mean he didn't want to, though. He cast another look at Sophia; the realization that he wanted to make sure she was okay was an odd one. He'd only known her for two hours at best and yet he empathized with her completely.

"They were reported missing today," he said, squaring his shoulders. Richard's brow furrowed, his frown deepened. Braydon balled his fists again, his body winding up. "This is why you let us know when something like this happens. This is why you call the police. It doesn't matter if you're taking time off of your job to locate Miss Hardwick because it's *my full-time job* to do that. I help people for a living, Richard." Braydon wasn't yelling. In fact, his voice had taken on an eerie calm. That calm voice indicated how furious he was that Richard had not reported the disappearance of Lisa. The missing woman who had a sibling drowning in a sea of worry—one beautiful woman desperate for answers. Professionalism was dialing his volume back but it wasn't diluting his intensity. "Now let me do my job and tell me everything else you found out or I'll arrest you for impeding an investigation."

It turned out that Richard was almost as clueless as they were. Apart from the cell phone, he hadn't found any evidence of blatant foul play or anything that pointed to Lisa running away. He had instead kept eyes and ears out for the woman he loved, hoping above all else that everything had been a misunderstanding. She hadn't run. She hadn't been taken. Braydon knew better than to cling to such false hope. If someone dropped off the face of the earth for four days, there was something wrong. Like kicking an addiction, admitting there was a problem was the first step.

Richard Vega hadn't handled that step well.

They wasted little time in unnecessary back-and-forth before Braydon told Richard he needed to see the exact place where the cell phone had been recovered. As far as they knew, it was the last place Lisa had been—tied by electronic tracking and hard evidence. If he could see it with his own eyes, then maybe he could see more of what had happened through hers.

"Am I riding with you or him?" Sophia asked as Richard pulled his car out of the garage. Like most houses on Loop Road it had more square footage than the resident had known what to do with.

"You can ride with either," Braydon said, watching Richard for any signs of fleeing. He didn't think the wealthy man would run, but he couldn't be too sure he wouldn't. Just because the whole town seemed to love the upstanding, well-groomed businessman, didn't mean Braydon was going to put his faith in Richard's good intentions. "We're all going to the same place."

Braydon walked over to the 370Z and inclined his head down to meet Richard's gaze.

"It should go without saying but if you try to leave or do anything suspicious, I'll find you and arrest you."

"I understand." He responded without hesitation. "I assure you that you now have my full cooperation."

"Good." Braydon patted the top of the car and went back to his truck. He was surprised to see Sophia already sitting in the cab with the air conditioner blasting. "How did you turn the car on?"

She remained still as she answered, her eyes closed in the cold air stream. "I used the key. You know, the things that people use to start cars?"

"Your sarcasm is noted, but what I meant was how did you get my keys?"

"You threw them on the dash here." She opened one eye, watching as he climbed into the driver's seat. "Not the best hiding place." He shifted into Drive and began following Richard out onto Loop Road.

"Tom says I have a nasty habit of doing that." Being a cop in Culpepper had seemed to activate an invisible barrier around the truck. No one wanted to steal or strip down his vehicle. The townspeople knew better. "That still doesn't give you the right to turn it on."

"Listen, it feels like it's over 100 degrees in this place. I needed some air and I needed it fast." She closed her eyes again and let the air conditioner push against her face. It was flushed from the heat, he could now tell. There were patches of red across her soft skin, though she was still attractive.

"That outfit isn't helping," he observed.

"And that is also noted."

They dove into a small silence. Sophia's perfume was slowly filling the space of the cab. He marveled at the contrast between its airy sweetness and her hard resolve.

"I'm surprised you didn't want to ride with Richard," Braydon admitted. "I thought you two would want to catch up." She had picked him, a stranger, over someone she knew of and who had close ties with her sister. Plus, that man had been Richard Vega. He could charm his way out of a jail cell faster than Braydon could lock the door. Another reason why he hadn't yet arrested the man. Though, he would in a heartbeat if he needed to.

Sophia snorted.

"Remember when I said Lisa and I weren't on the best terms this past year?" She motioned to the sports car in front. "Meet Richard Vega. He was the hammer to our nail."

Braydon glanced over at her. "What happened?"

Sophia turned her head so fast that her bun released the rest of her hair. "It's none of your business," she snapped.

"It is if you want me to find your sister, I need *all* of the details pertaining to her and Richard." Her anger seemed to fade.

"Why? Do you think Richard had something to do with her disappearance?"

Braydon thought about it before he answered. Richard certainly had the means to make a person fall off the radar but there had been an unmistakable concern that had covered every word and movement when he spoke of Lisa. "I personally think the only thing he's guilty of is being a prideful son of a bitch, but I don't want to rule him out, either. So, if there was a fight between all of you, there could potentially be a motive."

She went back to fidgeting with her hands.

"I really don't think that has anything to do with what's happening…."

"A good detective can't leave clues half-uncovered." He prodded with a gentler tone, "If we're going to find your sister, I need all of the information."

She put her hand up to the vent and quieted. The past wasn't a pleasant place to frequent, he knew that, but sometimes it was a necessity. He remained patient and watched as Richard turned off Loop Road and onto a connector that would get them to the main one. His red little car could easily outrun the truck. Braydon imagined the only reason he was going the speed limit was to avoid pissing him off any more.

Sophia sighed, touching her face with her now-cold hand.

"It was over money," she started. "And we never really had a fight. It was more of a buildup of things we *didn't* say. My dad died when we were little and Mom worked full-time while doing odd jobs along the way to support us. The years went by and we could see her trying to not blame us for her having to work so hard, but eventually the resentment set in. Lisa and I picked up the slack and looked out for one another—encouraged good grades, gave each other rides to work and helped take care of everything else. Lisa was my older sister, but she didn't raise me—we raised each other." Her voice shook and Braydon had to look to see if she was crying. Her head was bent, her fingertips suddenly fascinating. "Lisa has always been the prettier, more charming sister. As we got older, she was handed more opportunities, but she never really took them. That is until she started dating Richard. He offered her a world on a gold platter and she just took it. No questions asked. We spent years working so hard to make something of ourselves and then it was like she took the easy way out." Her voice softened. "We never fought about it—I never said those exact words—but she picked up on how I felt."

"And that was?"

"Anger...with a touch of resentment." Her face flushed red. "Saying it out loud seems stupid, especially now with everything going on. I should be happy for her, but Richard was just a hard pill to swallow, I suppose. Still, I don't think that has anything to do with her disappearance. The times we did talk this past year, she seemed genuinely happy."

Again, Braydon was surprised by the woman next to him. Just like that she had not only told him a personal story, but she had admitted her true feelings about it. He understood her stubbornness; however, it was the ease at which she told the truth that made the younger Hardwick sister more and more intriguing.

"Does your mother know about Lisa, then?" He couldn't remember her bringing the woman up in detail before. Surely she would have been there.

"No." She didn't elaborate and Braydon didn't push her. The way her body tensed like the string on a bow, he knew he had hit a deep nerve. Her openness apparently had its limits.

"What about you, Detective? Any family drama to share?" Sophia said it as a joke, something to lighten the dark mood, but she couldn't have picked a worse topic. Years of experience saved his composure. He smiled and shook his head.

"Nothing worth talking about."

Chapter Three

Richard took them west on Highway 20, following the slight curve of the two-lane until they passed Tipsy's Gas & Grill on the left. Sophia was surprised at the appearance of "One of the Best Eats in Culpepper" gas station/eatery. It was bigger than she had imagined—the original convenience store attached to another building, twice its size. She didn't know if it was the city girl in her, but she hadn't expected it to look as cozy as it did. Her stomach growled at the idea of Tipsy's advertised fried shrimp. The last thing she had eaten was a granola bar the night before.

They drove a few miles past Tipsy's before Richard turned on his blinker and pulled to the shoulder. Thatcher followed, the moment of vulnerability on Sophia's part gone. Why had she given him so much detail about Lisa and herself? Why did he need to know about their childhood or the fact that a part of her had started to resent Lisa? Maybe it was sleep deprivation. She hadn't been able to sleep all that well since Richard had called.

That was it. She'd blame it on that and not the mysterious man next to her.

Richard pointed at the tall grass a few feet from the road. They followed him, examining the area around it for something he might have missed. There was nothing.

"I'm going to call over a car and have them sweep farther back." Thatcher walked to his truck and pulled out the radio to make the call. Sophia and Richard kept to the grass.

"I'm sorry," he said, using his foot to move some rocks around. If it was meant to make him look vulnerable, it wasn't working. "I should have kept you updated. I was too caught up in finding her."

"You should have called the cops."

"Sophia, just because I chose not to call them doesn't mean I didn't have people looking for her."

"You mean the private investigators?"

"They aren't the only ones."

Sophia gave him a questioning look.

"I'm a very wealthy man with a lot of friends. I have contacts that operate outside of the police purview." He turned his body so his back was facing the cars. "I know people who don't get stopped by red tape."

"What does that mean?"

"Cops sometimes slow down investigations."

"I don't understand what you're trying to tell me." Sophia crossed her arms over her chest. The tip of her heels sunk into the ground. "You don't want the cops looking for Lisa because you have 'friends'?"

He made a frustrated noise.

"I'm just saying, there are reasons why I didn't call the police in the first place."

"You said you didn't call because you thought she just ran off?" A feeling of alarm was starting to rise within her. "Are you saying you *knew* she didn't just leave?"

There was the underlying implication again. A man with that much money, good looks and charm—though she didn't see it—could get away with a lot. If he had "friends" like he claimed, couldn't he use them to help him... Help him what? Dispose of Lisa?

Just thinking it sent a chill through Sophia.

"No, it's just— We were so happy, Sophia. I didn't think she just left."

Sophia dropped down to a whisper, eyeing Thatcher's back as he talked to the dispatcher.

"You lied to us," she said in a rush.

"I didn't lie. There was a moment where I wondered if she had gone on her own accord but, you know your sister, she wouldn't do that." She felt her defenses flare—of course she knew her sister. Even though they had grown apart didn't mean she had forgotten her.

"So, who are these friends of yours? Where are they?"

"All you need to know is that they are doing whatever they need to do to find Lisa." He stopped there and didn't make any sign of elaborating other than maybe using the whole "I've already said too much" excuse for keeping silent. In his black suit, the sun shining bright around them, Richard Vega looked a lot more threatening than he had in his home. He was shorter than Thatcher but had a solid body frame with muscles hidden beneath his custom-made suit, a gift from his personal trainer no doubt. Sophia wasn't a string bean or anything. She had muscles, too. They were just a little harder to see. Work had become hectic in the past two years. Going to the gym had been low on her priority list. That didn't mean she was completely defenseless.

Now, standing so close to a man she hardly knew but was admitting freely that he had connections that didn't pay heed to law enforcement, she was second-guessing if she could really hold her own and defend herself if needed.

Maybe her face showed the new sense of trepidation she was feeling. Thatcher tilted his head slightly to the side when their eyes met. His own expression was heavily guarded.

"A car should be here soon. They'll sweep this area again and then go farther back, just to make sure," he said. "If there's anything out here, they'll find it."

He brought his gaze to Richard now. There was no mistaking he was in detective mode—his feet spread apart, his back straight as a board, determination seeping through his stance.

"Now," he went on, "I'm going to have to ask you to come down to the station, Mr. Vega."

Richard seemed taken aback. Anger flashed across his face.

"I've already told you everything. Shouldn't we be using our time more wisely?"

Thatcher crossed his arms. Sophia couldn't help but think about how handsome he was in that moment. No-nonsense, authoritative, and all wrapped within a rock-hard body. She would have liked to meet Braydon Thatcher under different circumstances.

"Richard, I'm not giving you a choice. You're coming to the station." Thatcher pointed to his sports car. "The only decision you have to make is which car you ride in to get there."

Sophia rode with Thatcher again as they went back to the station. Richard had opted to ride in his car, barely keeping his cursing below his breath, while the detective had spent a good five minutes once again warning him against fleeing.

"Are you going to arrest him?" Sophia asked as soon as they pulled onto the highway.

"Yes."

"Why? Can you do that?" Sophia asked, adjusting the

air so that it was blowing on her face again. Florida heat didn't agree with her. Thatcher's teeth ground together, his jaw muscles clenching. Whatever he had learned had upped his aggravation level exponentially.

"We just got word that a colleague of Vega's has been going around asking people about Lisa, using the man's name as an unofficial police badge." He turned to her, nostrils flared. "That's impeding an investigation."

Sophia jumped up and down in her seat once. It caught Thatcher off guard but she didn't care. She repeated her recent conversation with Vega. It didn't improve his mood. When they pulled into the station's parking lot, he turned to her with a silent ferocity.

"I want you to go in there and answer every question we have about your sister." Having been given the instruction made her want to run the other way, but she knew it had to be done. "And, Sophia." He grabbed her hand. "I swear to you that I'll find your sister and bring her back safely."

The station seemed to stand at attention when Richard Vega walked in with Thatcher close behind, watching with expressions of interest mixed with disbelief. Even Cara looked up from her computer as the two men marched into the interrogation room.

Sophia wanted to follow them but doubted Richard would say anything else without an attorney—one dressed to the nines and with a bank statement that would be too good for the town of Culpepper. She instead was guided into Thatcher's office where she sat with a sigh. Back to the drawing board, she thought, crossing her legs like the dignified woman she hoped she appeared to be.

"Give us a minute," Detective Langdon said, popping out of the room before she could object. It wasn't as if she had any pressing matters to deal with or anything.

Just because she had bonded with Thatcher during their field trip didn't mean her impatience would keep its head down. She waited for a few minutes, with tried calmness, until only Thatcher breezed in.

His thick eyebrows were furrowed—his lips thinned in contained anger. He sat down behind his desk and ran a hand through the dark mass of hair. The obvious frustration he was feeling put Sophia further on edge.

"Well?" she prompted. "What did Richard have to say?"

"That he won't say anything else until his attorney arrives." Well, she called that one. "But, I hadn't expected anything different. With the amount of money that man has, I'm surprised he even talked to us as much as he did." A sigh rumbled out.

"So, what now? Do you want me to go talk to him? I can try to—"

Thatcher held up his hand to silence her.

"Right now you need to answer some questions about your sister."

"Fine."

They were able to slip into the civil roles of detective and citizen as Thatcher asked a series of questions that would help him form a "psychological profile" on Lisa. Even though they believed Lisa hadn't disappeared on her own accord, Thatcher had to still get a feel for the woman's mental and emotional states as well as any health issues she might be experiencing. Sophia did her best to answer each question in an objective manner, but, the truth was, she couldn't be sure how happy Lisa had been before the disappearance. Nor could she tell the man in full confidence that her sister had been upset.

"In general Lisa has always been an optimist," she confessed. "She always smiled and had something nice to say growing up—compliments on the tip of her tongue at all times. It's part of the reason why she charms everyone she meets." Thatcher raised an eyebrow but lowered it before she continued. "Like I said before, the times I did talk with her she seemed genuinely happy while here in Culpepper."

"Was there a particular reason she moved to Culpepper?" Sophia sent him a questioning look. "I only ask because you said the two of you were very close until this past year."

A smile crept across her lips before she could stop it.

"Her moving to Culpepper had nothing to do with our relationship. Lisa and I were the best of friends—annoyingly inseparable." Sophia hesitated on the past tense and sobered. "But Lisa hated Atlanta. I couldn't blame her for leaving. She was passing through Culpepper on the way to a wedding almost two years ago when she said she fell in love with the town. She moved a few months later."

"And you didn't follow?"

"No, but she tried really hard to get me to." Lisa had in fact boxed up Sophia's room while she'd been at work. She'd just smiled when Sophia had started yelling.

I'm not moving, Lisa!

Why not? Your stuff is already packed! she'd reasoned. Sophia had found it annoying then, but now she couldn't stop the ache in her heart.

"I don't blame her," Thatcher said under his breath.

"Excuse me?"

"Sorry, I meant I don't blame her for not liking the city. I'm not a big fan, either," he said with conviction.

"It's not too bad," Sophia defended. "It can be lonely at times and the traffic leaves more to be desired, but the opportunities are great."

"Lonely, huh? I take it you aren't married, then." It

wasn't a question and his eyes stayed down on his notes. Sophia picked at invisible lint on her pant leg and tried to keep her voice even.

"Not that it matters to this investigation but, no, I'm single." A blush rose fast to her cheeks. Thatcher looked up. She had only meant to say she wasn't married, not divulge that she was single and had bouts of loneliness.

"What about you?" Sophia wanted to stick her head in the sand. She had blurted the question in an attempt to save face. She had to give it to the detective, he answered without skipping a beat.

"No, I'm not married. Now, are there any health issues Lisa has that we should be worried about?" The change in subjects left her speechless for a moment, but still able to feel the heat in her cheeks, she finished the rest of his questions without any more awkward outbursts.

"The other two women who are missing..." she started after he closed his notebook.

"Amanda and Trixie."

"Are their families being asked the same questions?" Thatcher nodded.

"Amanda's mother and Trixie's boss are in the other rooms with Tom and Cara." His cell phone started to vibrate against the desktop. The noise made Sophia jump. He didn't notice as he read the message.

"What happens now that I've answered your questions?"

"Now we are going to go to each missing woman's house and place of work." He stood and stretched, his biceps rippling at the motion.

"All right." She started to stand but he stopped her.

"By 'we' I mean Detective Langdon and myself. You can't come this time and that's final."

"Then what do you want me to do? Sit here and twiddle my thumbs?"

"We have an all-points bulletin out on all three women. We have good men and women on the job, Miss Hardwick. You need to stay out of Lisa's house until we're done with the search but after that you can go wherever you please. There's a diner down the road that has a great dinner special or you can stay here until we're done with each search. It's really up to you at this point."

Sophia chewed the inside of her lip. Thatcher took her silence as compliance.

"I'll let you know when we're done at Lisa's."

The detectives left soon after while Sophia remained behind. She wanted to snoop to fill the void of helplessness within her but decided against it—she was in a police station after all. Cara, as she was told once again to call the officer, showed her to the restroom and then the break room. Unlike the many cop-related clichés found on TV, there were no doughnuts or cream-filled pastries. Instead she walked a block over and ate a burger at Sal's Diner, all the while fighting the heat and humidity. Worry had taken her healthy eating habits and thrown them clear out the window. The walk back was more sluggish but she couldn't deny she felt better having eaten.

An unfamiliar car was parked two spots next to her own when she rounded the station, though it didn't take long for her to guess it belonged to Richard's attorney. The BMW was black and slick and probably worth more than she made in two years. She hurried inside to see the new suit but was stopped by another man she hadn't seen until now.

"Miss Hardwick," he said, extending his hand. "I'm Captain Jake Westin." They shook—his hands were rough and large.

"Nice to meet you, sir." The man wasn't much taller than Sophia, but he exuded authority through his uniform and impeccable posture. She placed his age in the upper fifties.

"I wanted to let you know that we're doing everything we can and we'll find your sister." His small smile wasn't charming but it was infused with confidence. She nodded and thanked him. "I'm afraid I can't talk long. I have a meeting with Mr. Vega and his attorney."

"I understand," she said before shaking his hand once more. Though his grip was solid, she couldn't help but compare it to Detective Thatcher's. "Let me know if I can do anything to help."

"Will do." He turned and then disappeared into the conference room—all blinds were closed over the windows. If Cara and another cop hadn't been in the room with her, Sophia would have pressed her ear against the door to listen.

The Florida sun raged on as the hours dwindled into night before Sophia finally left the station. She had stayed around to see what would happen with Richard, but Captain Westin hadn't come out of the room by the time Thatcher had called to give the okay to go back to Lisa's house. She had even waited another half hour but decided it was a lost cause for the moment. With Richard's attorney in there, the man had probably not even spoken yet. She said a quick goodbye to Cara and headed to her car.

Sophia's adrenaline from the day's events was also on the decline. She hadn't lost her drive to find Lisa, in fact it felt stronger than ever knowing even Captain Westin was personally involved, but she couldn't deny the weight of exhaustion settling on her shoulders.

She was practical enough to realize that she was no

help to her older sister if she was constantly battling the droop of her eyelids.

Lisa lived in Pebblebrook, a neighborhood on the outskirts of town. It was a community of nice brick houses, man-made ponds and flowers galore. There always seemed to be a mother and her children walking the seemingly unending sidewalks—geared up to lose weight and release toddler-induced stress. When Lisa had moved into the neighborhood two years before, she hadn't been able to hide her happiness. It was a giant leap above her last apartment.

Sophia drove on autopilot deeper into Pebblebrook's belly with the soft sounds of a local talk radio show in the background. Since she didn't have as much to contribute in the ways of police detection, she was already forming a proactive to-do list in her head.

Check Lisa's house more thoroughly.

Go to Lisa's work and search for a work schedule or appointment books.

Get an update from Detective Thatcher—

Her train of thought derailed. Thatcher's voice when he promised to find her sister blanketed the ever-present fear inside her, comforting Sophia for the moment. She believed his sincerity—it was strong and determined. His blue eyes had pierced her own with a ferocity to undo all of the bad and replace it with the good. The reaction had been a lot more than Sophia had expected from the small-town detective.

However, the fact remained, Lisa was *her* sister, not his. He hadn't grown up with her, cared for her, been there at the lowest points in life or the highest. He didn't know that her favorite movie was *The Little Mermaid* or that she was deathly afraid of owls. He didn't know about the scar across her ankle that she had gotten from falling off a swing set when she was nine or that, despite their rocky childhood, she had always been kind to their mother. Detective Thatcher didn't know Lisa, so he couldn't love her the way Sophia did.

No matter how dedicated he was to his job, he would never have the drive she had to make sure Lisa was found.

It was almost six by the time she pulled into 302 Grandview Court. The street was the farthest from the entrance to Pebblebrook, all houses backed up a thick stretch of woods, and all Sophia could hear were insects and frogs—the music of the South. The loud but subtle sound annoyed her, as it always had. In the city there were still the sounds of insects but car horns and loud neighbors drowned them out. Here, there were no such distractions.

Lisa lived in a single-family home that was a mix between contemporary and ranch-style. Alternating shades of beige and brown brick wrapped around the three-bedroom, two-bath home while a well-tended garden lined the entryway. Sophia didn't know how Lisa had kept the plants alive and healthy. If it had been her garden, there would be more weeds than flowers and a lot less color—she just didn't have enough patience to have a green thumb. The inside of the house, admittedly, made Sophia a little green with envy.

The entryway led past an open front room and into an open-floor-plan kitchen, dining area and living room. Off the kitchen was a hallway with the two guest bedrooms and a full bath; off the living room was the very large master bedroom and en suite. Plus a walk-in closet that was bigger than Sophia's bedroom in her apartment. It wasn't enough that the house was large, but it was also *upgraded*. Granite countertops, dark-wood cabinets, vaulted-and-tray ceilings with exposed wooden beams, and hardwood throughout. The house had been done to the nines. It was beautiful.

Sophia felt a stab of guilt as the green monster inside poked his nose up into the air. She should be happy that her sister lived in such a nice house—that she had such a nice life. However, Sophia couldn't swallow the lump that Richard had had a hand in securing the house. It would have been different if he also lived there but he stayed in his mansion on Loop Road. Sophia may have lived in a tiny apartment but it was a tiny apartment she had *earned,* not been handed. Lisa, although older, had always skirted the line of earning things versus being handed them—something made easier by her good looks and charm.

Sophia sighed.

This was an old fight between the Hardwick sisters, a useless, petty one now that Lisa was missing.

Sophia grabbed her duffel and changed into a striped tank top, blue jeans and a pair of Nikes. Relinquishing the heels and stuffy pantsuit was a welcomed feeling. There was no boss here that she was trying to impress, no promotion she was chasing with professional work wear and impeccable posture. She was in a safe zone—one lacking work-related worry yet lined with stress-induced questions about Lisa's future.

Packing had been quick and careless. She noticed the absence of her shampoo, razor and sleep clothes, though they hadn't seemed too important at the time. She wondered if it was a note about her character that she hadn't forgotten her work laptop. She rummaged through the bag until she found her cell phone charger. It wasn't like anyone was anxiously awaiting her to text or call but with Lisa out there, she wanted it to at least be fully charged.

She plugged the ancient phone into a wall socket before stretching wide.

Even though sleep had been a rational thought, Sophia couldn't bring herself to settle down. All notions of getting some rest had evaporated. Instead she found the coffee and thanked the high heavens that there was enough creamer left for one cup. One very large cup. With the silky goodness sliding down her throat and warming her belly, she decided to search the house again.

She went through each room much slower than when she had first blown into town, searching high and low for any clue that could peg a time frame or place Lisa had gone to. The detectives left the house in the same order they had found it, thankfully, and this time around she was able to note the details—the decorations that made the house innately Lisa's.

The front room had been set up as an office. A desk and bookcase lined one wall while a bright blue love seat sat opposite. From first glance there was nothing that screamed, "This is where I went and this is who took me!" There was also no laptop, just a pristine area of minimal clutter.

Sophia opened the desk drawers and searched its contents. She found coupons for a clothing store two cities over, enough sticky notes to create a note-taking army, and bundles of multicolored pens scattered throughout. Lisa had always loved what she called "nontraditional" pens.

"They dare to be different!" she would say after signing a check with electric-green ink or writing her name in a birthday card with an annoyingly loud shade of fuchsia. It was a habit she had picked up in grade school and hadn't been able to shake since. When Sophia was little she had been so angry with her sister that she'd replaced the colorful pens for a ten-pack of black and blues. To this day she had never seen Lisa so angry. The then-girl had turned such a bright shade of red, she would have probably liked to add it to her collection of odd inks.

Sophia took care to shut the drawers without snapping or pinching the writing utensils. If Lisa came back to find them busted open it would be another round of older-sibling rage…. She paused. *When* Lisa came back.

Picture frames and knickknacks lined the bookcase. From little elephant figurines to frozen scenes of Lisa, Sophia, friends she didn't know and even Richard. The two of them were pressed together in an intimate hug—both smiling, both happy. Another pang of jealousy twisted in her stomach. She physically tried to tamp it down with her hand. There was no time or reason for her to be envious again.

The guest bedrooms were also unhelpful. They both housed a bed and night tables but were neat and orderly—no one had stayed in them recently. The guest bathroom told the same story as well as the pantry and refrigerator. Both were barely stocked. She moved through the living room, warily eyeing the yellow sectional and glass coffee table that was decorated with neon-colored candles, and once again was met with the master suite.

If ever a room could capture the essence of Lisa Gale Hardwick, it was this room. The walls were a light pink that traveled up and across the double-tray ceiling while white trim lined the two windowsills on either side of the bed. That bed. It was a king-size, another luxury Sophia hadn't been able to experience yet, covered in a loud pink silk comforter with flowers of varying sizes sewn in. There were six fuzzy pillows piled high, all neon green, yellow, orange and pink. They were soft to the touch. Sophia smiled.

She remembered how annoyed she used to be at Lisa's love for pillows. Even though their bedroom was small and they each had a twin-size bed, there always seemed to be more pillows than bedroom. The older Hardwick would pile them high during the day only to throw them on the floor between their beds during the night. It had driven Sophia crazy.

But you'll sure thank me if you roll out of bed while you're asleep, she would say. If that didn't appease the younger, grumpier girl, Lisa would go as far as to demonstrate by rolling out of bed. She would laugh as the pillows cushioned the fall. *See? I'm kind of brilliant.* If this second attempt still didn't work, she would tug Sophia down with her. No matter her mood, this always did the trick. She would laugh and feel the sisterly bond that connected them. Over the years it became a skit between them—an inside joke. Sophia hadn't realized how much she missed those moments until now, staring at a much bigger bed, standing in a much bigger room.

Her lips went slack, the smile fading. She put the pillow back, wanting to stop the trip down memory lane and find the lost woman instead. If there were no clues to find in the house, she would just have to continue the search elsewhere.

The coffee was doing its wonderful job. It pumped energy throughout Sophia's body like water down a twisty slide. The heaviness in her eyelids had been replaced by an almost nervous twitch as she hopped into her car and drove down the road, fingers drumming against the steering wheel along with an alternative rock song she didn't quite know and her mind set on Details. Most of Culpepper were getting into bed, their heads heavy but hearts happy that Friday was only a deep sleep away.

The rest of the house search had been uneventful.

There were no hints or clues to where Lisa had gone or why, but Sophia hadn't been too surprised—the house looked barely lived in. If there was anything she had left behind it was either at her work or at Richard's house. She didn't know how either search would go considering Richard and his motley crew of "friends" had probably already gone through both, but she wanted to try. Once she went through Details, she would be giving Richard a call.

The sound of buzzing made Sophia swerve. Her heart thudded hard as she reached for her cell phone, expectations high. An unknown local number flashed on the screen.

"Hello?" she answered, hope pouring through the sound.

"Sophia Hardwick?" The hope that her sister was on the other end of the line evaporated as the man answered.

"This is she."

"It's Detective Braydon Thatcher, sorry to call so late." A new feeling of alarm followed.

"Have you found Lisa?" She wanted and didn't want an answer. What if they *had* found her and she was—

"No, but we're working hard on that." She let out a breath. "I wanted to—" There was a pause. Sophia pulled the phone out to make sure the call hadn't dropped. "I just wanted to check in. How are you doing?"

That caught her off guard. She answered honestly.

"Frustrated. I also went through Lisa's house but didn't find anything. I'm heading over to her work right now to see if I can find *something*."

"We already went through Details," he said.

"Well maybe you missed something only I would pick up on."

"You know, you aren't supposed to go over there. I've already had to section it off because so many people think they are cops." There was no mistaking the anger that lined his tone. Though Richard seemed to be popular among most of Culpepper, that didn't seem to count for much in Detective Thatcher's book. "I can arrest you for going, you know. For impeding a police investigation."

"But I'm her sister!" she said in a rival degree of anger. "I have more right to be there than you!"

"Not by law, ma'am."

"Don't you 'ma'am' me!" If Thatcher hadn't been in law enforcement she would have hung up the phone then. No one was going to tell her what she could and couldn't do when it came to finding Lisa and they certainly weren't going to do it while calling her ma'am.

Maybe Thatcher realized she was ready to have an all-out verbal phone fight. He waited a beat before the sound of a heavy sigh escaped on his end.

"Fine, but go through the back door so you don't break the tape. I'm assuming you have a key?"

"Yes, *sir*."

"Call me if you find anything, but don't get your hopes up. We already swept that area thoroughly."

She bit her lip. "Fine. I'll call if I see anything."

They ended the call and Sophia tried to ignore that continued thud of her heart.

Details was housed in a small, narrow building that had once been home to a florist's shop.

"It's the perfect fit, Sophy!" Lisa had exclaimed after the first walk-through. "I don't even have to change the colors!"

She sure was right about that. The outside brick concealed an inside of varying shades of blue and yellow that popped from natural light from the mostly glass front waiting room. Details was attached to a home decor store dedicated to everything wood. Lisa had told her that the couple who owned it were "more religious than God himself" but that information was neither here nor there for Sophia. She was on a mission to find something, anything that would help her locate her sister.

Like Detective Thatcher ordered, she pulled out her key and walked around back. She knew this building as well as she knew Lisa's house. It was the whole boyfriend area that she had missed out on. She moved through the building, checking the lobby, Lisa's office, the break room and the bathroom. It was ridiculously neat. If there were any colored pens they were hiding. What's more, she couldn't find anything that resembled a calendar or appointment book that could help peg where and when she had gone.

That seemed like a clue in itself but she refrained from calling Thatcher to tell him so. Instead, after an hour of searching high and low, she admitted defeat and drove back to Pebblebrook, yawning the entire way there. The cup of coffee had been big, but not big enough.

SOPHIA DIDN'T HAVE the heart to move the pillows aside when she decided she needed a few hours of sleep. Without her older sister's giggles or beaming smile as she threw one pillow after the other to the ground, it didn't seem worth the effort. She grabbed a blanket from the hall closet and made the couch her target instead.

She tried to sleep with all of her might, but worries plagued her thoughts. A few minutes of rolling around turned into an hour before she decided sleeping couldn't happen yet. What she needed was something to snack on but after going through the pantry and refrigerator again she came up empty. Another defeat to add to the growing list of disappointments.

"You don't even have some crackers, Lisa," she said aloud. "I would have been happy with only a few."

She stood back and patted her stomach, uncertain of her next move. The sound of the lock turning from the back door sounded like a bomb going off in the silent kitchen. She whirled around as hope sprung through her so violently that she stumbled backward. It had to be Lisa. It just had to be.

Before she could run to greet the long-haired beauty, the door opened to reveal a man Sophia didn't recognize. A grin split open his face. He shut the door behind him and flipped the lock.

Sophia may not have been perfect under pressure, but she had enough sense to grab a knife from the holder on the counter. She brandished it like a sword and tried not to scream.

Chapter Four

Sophia held the knife tight—both hands clasped around the grip. She didn't know if it was sharp but it sure didn't look dull. The blade was almost as long as her forearm. If this man came at her, he'd be the first to know how easily it could cut through skin.

"Who are you?" she asked, a noticeable tremor in her voice. "What are you doing in my house?"

The man walked into full view, a missing front tooth showing a dark, endless void.

"You aren't Lisa Hardwick," he stated. "This isn't your house."

"But I am her sister." Her grip was so tight on the knife, her hand hurt.

The man laughed, and thankfully kept his distance.

"I know who you are, Sophia. You put my employer in jail."

"Your employer?"

"Vega."

"You aren't the one who took Lisa?" His smile dropped. It was unnerving to see the stranger lose whatever humor he had.

"No, ma'am. I was hired to find her and bring her home safe."

Sophia eyed him warily.

"You can put the knife down. I have a gun in the back of my pants. If I wanted to kill you I would have done it by now." Sophia's stomach flip-flopped as he pulled the handgun out to show her before putting it back into the waist of his pants. "I was supposed to update Vega but seeing as he's in jail, I'm reporting to you."

That got Sophia's attention. She lowered her arm but kept the knife in hand.

"Do you know where she is?"

He shook his head. "But I found her car."

BRAYDON WAS STARING down into his never-ending cup of coffee. He'd already been getting bad sleep the past few days. Now time was starting to blur for him—he couldn't remember the last night he'd slept solidly. Tom and Officer Whitfield had stayed with him after all of the searches, going through phone records, financial reports, and trying to pinpoint where the women had last been before they'd disappeared. He was paying most attention to where Lisa had gone. He told himself it was because she had been the first to go missing, but a part of him knew the focus had been forged out of sympathy for Sophia Hardwick. No matter the motives behind the search, nothing was fitting together. No new evidence had popped up during the women's house searches or work searches. Aside from Richard's admission of tampering with potential crime scenes and withholding information, they didn't have any other leads.

Braydon took another long pull on his coffee. He knew he needed sleep—it would make him think better, but he couldn't bring himself to try. That would be valuable search time he would be wasting. Lisa, Trixie and Amanda couldn't afford for him to catch up on beauty sleep.

Sophia couldn't afford it, either.

Thinking of her, of her determination to find Lisa, was enough to push him into his third wind. He went over to the map of Culpepper stretched across the wall and looked at the locations of interest. All three women lived as far away from each other as possible. Lisa lived at the back end of Pebblebrook; Trixie lived on the opposite side of town in a house that was tucked away in the middle of some acreage; and Amanda lived with her mother in a house that backed up to the bay. His eyes stuck to the Alcaster tack on the map.

After all of these years, it was once again a part of an investigation. He just hoped this time it didn't involve a murder.

His concentration started to lose traction as he thought about Amelia—her vibrant smile, her infectious laugh... and her bloody corpse. It sent a familiar fire through him. If he had only been there sooner, if he had only protected her like he had promised when they were young, Terrance Williams wouldn't have had the chance to kill her.

He punched the top of his desk, his thoughts turning turbulent.

"Braydon." Tom knocked on the side of the opened office door. He craftily ignored the anger that was seeping out of his partner and waved with a phone in his hand. "You left this in the conference room. It's Sophia Hardwick."

"Thanks." He grabbed his phone and tried to tuck back into his normal self. He took a few breaths before answering. "Thatcher here."

"I know where Lisa's car is!" the woman all but screeched.

"What? How?"

"A man broke into the house and—"

"A man broke into the house? Are you okay? Is he still

there?" Braydon put his gun back into its holster, grabbed his keys and started to leave the station. He motioned to Tom to follow him.

"I'm fine. He's gone. He works for Richard. He was one of the 'friends' he told me about."

That relieved Braydon, but only a bit.

"Where's the car, then?"

"I'll tell you when you pick me up." There was that stubbornness weaving into her voice.

"Sophia," he warned.

"I promise I'll tell you when you get here. I don't want you to leave me behind, Detective. Now please hurry so we can go see if it's true."

"Fine, but lock yourself in a room and wait for us to get there."

"He's not coming back," she said. Braydon blew out an irritated breath.

"Sophia, three women in town have already disappeared. A man just broke into the house. Unless you have him chained up in the garage, I want you to go into a room and lock yourself inside. Do you understand me?"

There was a pause. He may not have known Sophia that well but he bet she was currently rolling her eyes. She finally sighed and said, "Okay."

Braydon had a patrol car closest to Pebblebrook search for a suspicious person while Tom followed behind to Lisa's. The heightened sense of urgency, he realized, wasn't for Lisa or the other missing women, but for Sophia. He didn't know how someone he barely knew had gotten so far under his skin, like a plant that had taken root years ago. He did, however, know that he had to protect her.

The drive to Lisa's would normally take ten minutes—Braydon got there in five.

"I'll secure the perimeter," Tom said as they met on the sidewalk. "You go check the house." They both pulled out their guns, Tom disappearing around the house, Braydon slowly opening the front door. He was going to go straight to the bedroom, thinking she would most likely hide there, when a crash from the kitchen snagged his attention. He rounded the corner with his gun raised.

"Sophia!" He found the woman standing over a broken glass. She jumped at his appearance.

"What are you pointing a gun at me for?" she said, face reddening.

"What are you doing in the kitchen? I thought I told you to lock yourself in a room. The front door wasn't even locked!"

"I was about to go to the bedroom but I was thirsty! And I left the front door unlocked so you could get in without breaking it down. Lisa would kill me if she came home and her door was destroyed." She put her hands on her hips. "Can you please put that thing away?" She motioned to the gun still raised in his hand. "It's not like I'm armed or anything." It was his turn to roll his eyes.

"You are a very maddening woman," he said. "Do you know that?"

"I've been told I'm difficult."

He put the gun back into its rightful place against his side. "Now stay here while I search the rest of the house." Braydon could tell she was about to argue, so he put up his hand to stop it. "Just let me do this."

She surrendered. "Fine by me."

The house was clean, he noted once again, as he searched each room and closet. It was also empty. There were no broken windows, doors or any signs of a break-in. The man hadn't used force to get in, that was for sure.

"All clear?" Sophia asked when he finished his round.

She put down a dustpan to get the remainders of the glass. Without thinking he crouched down to hold it. If the act surprised her like it did him, she didn't show it. Instead she swept the rest of the shards in without commenting.

"Were all the doors locked before he showed up?" he asked.

She nodded as he moved the pan back so she could get to the line of bits that never seemed to want to go in the first time. Braydon's house was all hardwood. He knew what a pain it was to sweep. "Of course I did. I doubled-checked all of the windows and doors. He either picked the lock or..." She stiffened a fraction.

"Or what?"

"I think he had a key."

Braydon stopped, the dustpan in his hand.

"A key?"

"It makes sense—I don't remember hearing anything weird like someone working on a lock. He unlocked it with ease. He *did* say that Richard hired him to find Lisa. I guess he gave him a way to get into the house."

That didn't sit right with Braydon. His brow furrowed. Sophia put the broom down and took the dustpan from his hand. Their fingers brushed. They paused in unison. Electricity coursed between their touching skin. Whether it was a desire to protect the black-haired beauty or something more sensual than that, he wasn't sure. She looked up at him through her long lashes. There was a feeling that flickered behind her deep green eyes, but he couldn't place what. Sophia cleared her throat and took a step away.

"But, I—that's not what we should be focusing on here," she said, emptying the pan into the trash can.

"I don't know about that, but we'll revisit this topic." Tom came in then and reported the lot was clear. He said a quick hello to Sophia before she led them into the living room. Barely veiled excitement propelled her forward—a bounce lining each step—the moment between them in the kitchen short-lived.

"The man, and before you ask he didn't give a name, went through Lisa's office and found something we all missed." She handed him a Post-it note. "He said it had fallen between the desk and the trash can. Do you know where this is?"

Braydon froze. It read Dolphin Lot.

He knew *exactly* where it was.

Chapter Five

Sophia didn't have to know the men all that well to know something was off. Instead of immediately jumping into the cars to go to Dolphin Lot, there was a mass hesitation. Tom was staring at Thatcher while he stared at the note. She didn't understand the cause of the silence attached, either. Lisa had been missing for five days—locating her car was a lead she was happy to have found...or rather, been given.

"So, you do know where the Dolphin Lot is?" she prodded when neither man answered her first question. Thatcher nodded. He didn't elaborate. Sophia looked to Tom for answers.

"Braydon and I were actually near there the morning you showed up."

"Well, great! Then we can go there now." Tom cast a quick look at Thatcher, concerned. Sophia didn't understand why everything had suddenly slowed down. This was the first real clue they had. She was about to say as much when Thatcher folded the note and put it in his pocket.

"I guess I can't get you to stay here," he said to her. His voice was flat, cold. It was such a drastic change from his earlier tone that she took an involuntary step back. Thatcher noticed the movement and tried on a small smile. Sophia wasn't buying it.

"No. For good or for bad I want to be there," she said. "I *need* to be there."

The detectives looked at each other, passing a message with their eyes, until Thatcher nodded. "Fine but only after you give us a brief description of the man who gave you this note."

Sophia held her temper and described the man's appearance to Tom as best she could.

"Are you going to arrest him? Shouldn't we have as many people as possible out there looking for these women?"

"What would be more helpful is if we were all on the same page," Thatcher was quick to answer. His jawline had set so hard that Sophia bet she could wield it as a weapon if she wanted.

Though, she couldn't disagree with the truth of what he said.

The detectives sent out the man's description to all of the on-duty cops. Sophia doubted they could catch the missing-tooth man. Even if he had a key, he had still caught her off guard. Plus, if Richard had hired him to "do whatever it takes" to find Lisa, then maybe it was better for everyone involved if he stayed elusive.

Sophia went through the familiar motions of getting into the passenger side of Thatcher's truck. She had ridden in it so much in the past twelve or so hours that she was met with the scent of her perfume as she sat down. She caught herself wondering if Thatcher liked it…and if the scent had attached to him, as well. If someone was close enough to him, would they smell it and think he was taken? Would the aroma act as a barrier to keep women from trying to hit on him?

Sophia quite liked that idea.

"So where is Dolphin Lot?" she asked. They pulled out of the driveway and drove into the night. Lisa's next-door neighbors peeked out from their windows as Tom reversed in his car and followed. "There seemed to be some tension at the mention of it."

Thatcher shifted in his seat. He kept his eyes straight ahead.

"It backs up to the bay on the outskirts of town. It's an undeveloped piece of land, maybe five acres in total. The closest house belongs to the Alcasters."

Sophia gasped. "Amanda Alcaster?"

"Technically her mother, Marina, owns the house, but, yes, Amanda lives there, too." Before Sophia could completely process that, he continued. "What's more is Dolphin Lot is owned by Marina, as well."

"That can't be a coincidence, can it?"

"I don't have all of the information to make a conclusion either way," he said before adding, "but, no, I wouldn't chalk it up to that."

The car filled with a pregnant silence. Sophia didn't know what to think now. Why had Lisa written down that address? Had Amanda called her over for help? Or maybe she had lured her in? Maybe it had nothing to do with the disappearances. Maybe it *was* just a coincidence. There were too many unknowns and she was starting to feel the lack of sleep drag her senses down.

Now that the small mystery of why the detectives had such a reaction to the address was solved, the more troublesome mystery started to settle in. What would they find once they got to Dolphin Lot?

THIS WAS ALL too familiar. The winding dirt road, the blanket of darkness, the feeling of growing anxiety...

He had done this before. He had traveled down the same road, hitting every bump and dip in the dirt path, hurtling toward an uncertain future with a gun at his side. He had been here before.

Eleven years ago.

The difference now was that he wasn't alone. Sophia sat with her shoulders squared, lips thinned and hands back to fidgeting in her lap. Although she was looking at where the truck's headlights fell, he doubted she was seeing anything there. The happiness at finding a solid lead had ebbed away. She was worrying about her sister and what they would find now. He couldn't blame her one bit.

"This road will take us through the entire lot until it stops at the bay toward the end of the property," Braydon said. They turned with the road and crossed what he knew was the property line. "Those trees—" he pointed out her window "—divide the property in half. Tom will take the road that cuts across the field on the other side of them. We'll drive through first to see if we see anything, then we'll go out on foot."

Sophia nodded.

"I guess we got lucky with the weather," she said. "If it was cloudy we wouldn't be able to see anything."

She was right about that. The moon wasn't full but it was bright enough to allow them to see most of the field on each side. What would have been better was if they had found the sticky note during the day and not after midnight. The fact that they technically hadn't found the clue at all was a nuisance to his detective pride—he should have found the Post-it, not one of Richard Vega's hired thugs. He didn't have time to dwell on it too much. He needed to stay focused. He looked to his left while Sophia kept watch on the right. He wanted to keep her spirits high, but was having a hard enough time trying to push the past out of his thoughts.

Eleven years had passed. Terrance Williams wouldn't be back here. This might be familiar but there was no way it was the same as when he was eighteen. Braydon was thinking of ghosts when he needed to be focusing on finding Lisa. She had written the lot down for a reason, most likely to meet someone. If they could find her or why she had potentially gone there, then they might be closer to finding Trixie and Amanda, as well. He was still having a hard time swallowing that each disappearance wasn't connected. Like he told Sophia, he didn't buy that they were all coincidences.

"Are there any houses or buildings back here?" Sophia asked.

"No."

"Why not? If it backs up to the bay, I'd imagine you could sell it for a good amount." She was nervous, trying to distract herself, but she was closing in on bad territory. He may not want to talk about it, but Braydon didn't want to lie to her, either.

"Marina is a very superstitious woman. There was an incident here a while back where a man died." He shrugged, hoping his composure stayed firm. "She bought the land from the previous owner because she didn't want someone to build near her house but she refuses to touch the lot. Afraid of spirits and the like." The man hadn't been a good one and that was why she wouldn't build. Braydon kept that detail out, however.

"Hmm…" She went back to searching her side and Braydon attempted to ignore the growing anxiety in his chest. In less than two miles they would pass the area where the incident that changed his life all those years ago had taken place.

If the dock was his personal hell, that spot in the Dolphin Lot field was his personal devil.

"Does anyone come out here usually?" Sophia asked after a minute or two had passed.

"The occasional fisherman but only if they clear it with Marina. She'll call us if someone drives out here that she doesn't know. Out-of-towners don't usually know about it."

"I'm just trying to figure out why Lisa would be out here. She isn't the most outdoorsy kind of woman. One time she—"

Sophia may have been the most interesting woman Braydon had met in a long time, but he stopped listening to her halfway through. He slowed the truck involuntarily. Last time he had been here he had been so young and so angry. Ready to do what needed to be done. Ready to end a life. Now, as they neared the area, he kept his eyes to the left.

That's when he saw it.

He stopped the truck and radioed Tom.

"I need you to get over here, now."

Sophia turned and saw it, too. She took in a breath. "That's Lisa's car!"

"Where are you?" Tom asked.

Braydon clenched his teeth. There was no way it was a coincidence that Lisa's car was *there*.

"Right where Terrance Williams died."

"STAY IN THE CAR, SOPHIA" is something Thatcher would have probably said had she not thrown open the truck door and taken off running toward the car. He hadn't even finished his conversation with Tom but she didn't care. After days of not knowing anything, she finally had an answer. Although, Sophia knew that whatever was in the car wouldn't be an answer she wanted.

There were really only two ways it could go: the car would be empty or the car wouldn't be empty. The second option terrified her to her very core. The bright smile of Lisa Hardwick danced across her vision. Somewhere in the back of her mind she realized she might never see it again.

Sophia pushed through the thigh-high grass. Her adrenaline had spiked and at each step closer her stomach knotted tighter. Thatcher was yelling behind her but she didn't care. She needed to see what was or wasn't in the little green car.

The moonlight made it hard to see the small details around the vehicle when Sophia reached her destination, but all of the doors were shut and the windows intact. She let out a shaky breath. The front seats were empty. Her eyes roamed to the backseat. Her heart dropped with shattering speed. Without thinking, she opened the door and was hit with a wave of stench. It made her stomach roll, but not as much as the body lying across the seats.

Sophia stumbled back just as Thatcher caught up to her. His presence did nothing to stop the scream that tore from her throat.

Chapter Six

"Oh, Sophia." Braydon pulled the woman into his arms, walking her backward farther away from the car. He didn't have to look into it to know there was a decaying body inside. He could smell it. "I'm sorry. I'm sorry."

"No!" she cried into his shirt.

"Sophia." He held her close, knowing her grief. Years had dulled his own but he would never forget the original pain, like a wound that never healed—a puckered red scar that only he could see.

"No!" she yelled again, fisting her hands into his shirt. He was prepared to stand there, holding her, trying to console her as best he could, until Tom came. Seeing her sister's body would spike her emotions and make her irrational. He didn't want her to go back and look again. "No. It isn't—it isn't Lisa."

"What?" he said. She looked up, tears streaking her face.

"The body. She has blond hair." He knew he shouldn't have felt the slight relief that filled him now. There was still a woman in there. That someone had a family—a Sophia who cared—and wouldn't see them again. There should be no relief for someone else's death. "Go," she said, taking a shaky step back. "I'm—I'm okay."

"Are you sure?" He titled her chin up so he could

look squarely into her eyes. They shone bright green beneath the tears. An overwhelming desire to protect this woman consumed him. He wouldn't leave her side unless he knew she was okay and even then... He shook his head to clear any thoughts of the future. Right now he had to deal with the grim present.

"Yeah," she answered.

He nodded and gave her arm one last squeeze. "Stay here while I take a look, okay?"

"No problem."

Braydon switched on his flashlight and moved over to the car. If driving down the road had been familiar, then walking up to the car was downright déjà vu. The car in the clearing, the body in the backseat, the blood splattered against the back windshield. Braydon was on autopilot as he swept the light across the body. His mind raced. His palms became slick with sweat. The details weren't just similar but almost exact.

He had seen this before.

The body on its back, the gun pressed against the temple, a hole through the head where the bullet had traveled... It was the scene of suicide and, even though this time it was a woman in the same position, all Braydon could see was Terrance Williams.

HE WATCHED AS Braydon Thatcher, golden boy of the Culpepper PD, walked up to the car. Before the new detective even shone his flashlight over the body, he could see the tension that lined the man's shoulders. Braydon wasn't stupid. He knew what he would find inside. The detective had enough reason to not believe in so many coincidences.

Just like he had planned, Braydon's face contorted into

terrifying realization when he saw poor Trixie Martin with a gun up to her head.

It all made him smile.

He put his beer bottle back into the built-in cup holder of his chair. There were empty bottles scattered at his feet from the previous days. Waiting for Braydon to find the car had been a true test of his patience. One he had been afraid he would fail if he'd had to wait any longer. He was extremely thankful for the dispatch he'd picked up ten minutes before. Without hearing that Braydon was on his way to Dolphin Lot, he would have missed the entire show.

That would have been a pity. If Braydon had never found the car, then all of this would have been for nothing. He had worked too hard for the setup to go unseen.

Braydon's movements became clipped and clumsy while his mind, no doubt, worked through what was in front of him. The part of the puzzle he was meant to understand was laid out and rotting in that car while the "who" was a short, yet unconfirmed list. Eventually the man would fill in the blanks, but right now he was trying to maintain a professional neutrality with the crime scene and the woman shaking behind him.

That woman. She must have been Lisa's little sister, Sophia. They shared the dark hair but varied in height and curves. Whereas Lisa was a long-legged conventional beauty, Sophia was small and, dare he think it, cute—like a child playing dress up in adult clothing. He couldn't see the tears that spilled down her face from this vantage point within the cover of the trees, but he knew she was crying—her body shook in the humid night air.

Even though finding Trixie's body had been the main interest, he found Braydon's attention kept moving toward the woman. How the detective looked at her, how he held her, how he tried to console her... He felt something for her. He cared. This was a new development.

He took another pull on his drink. A new addition to the plan was forming. Sophia Hardwick was about to be reunited with her sister, though not under the circumstances that she wanted.

The idea was a catalyst to the smile that stretched across his face. It was time Detective Thatcher suffered the way he had all those years ago. It was time to show him that not all was forgotten.

The thought of his brother only hardened his resolve. He finished his drink and grabbed his bag. Right now Braydon was going through emotional shock but when that dissolved and the cop part of him kicked in, he would get suspicious of his surroundings—he would start looking for the culprit. It would be a shame for the detective to see him now.

That time was quickly approaching. Trixie's body was the first domino. Now, all he had to do was introduce himself to the second Miss Hardwick.

It was time to show Braydon that his entire life could be undone as easily as Terrance's had.

Chapter Seven

Detective Langdon showed up shortly after, racing at the insistence of his partner. He jogged to the car from the road, passing Sophia who had taken a moment to get sick off to the side. He, too, understood that the positioning and circumstances of Trixie's death, everything, right down to the spot on Dolphin Lot, was mimicked. The way he kept cutting his eyes toward Braydon spoke volumes.

"Who is it?" Sophia called from a distance. Her voice reminded Braydon that he needed to get back to the present and do his job. He focused on the woman's face and hair.

It was the blue-eyed, blond-haired Trixie Martin. Missing woman number two. She wore a tank top, running shorts and tennis shoes. Apart from the gunshot wound, the rest of her body seemed unharmed.

"I'm going to go call this in and get some backup here," Tom said just low enough for Braydon to hear. "Do you want to take Sophia home?"

"No. I want to go over the scene." He paused, then lowered his voice. "It's just how I found him all those years ago. This can't be a coincidence. The crime scene wasn't public knowledge. At least, not all of the details. Only a few of us saw it and Trixie Martin was nowhere near involved in it." Tom didn't respond. He didn't need to. There were only a handful of people who could have copycatted the death of Terrance Williams with such detail. Braydon's jaw hardened and he shook himself. "But send a car over to take her home." Tom nodded and started to turn around. "And tell them to watch her house." He couldn't shake the growing feeling of unease within him.

"You got it, Partner."

Braydon took another look at the young woman in the car before retreating to Sophia's side. Her expression tore at his heart. She had stopped crying but the concern and fear radiated off her in waves. More than anything, he felt the need to hold her and tell her everything was going to be okay. He would figure it out, he would find Lisa and Amanda, and he would bring justice crashing down on whoever was doing this.

"Who is it?" she asked again.

"Trixie Martin," he answered. "It's Trixie Martin."

Sophia sucked in a breath.

"And she killed herself? In my sister's car? But why?"

"Just because there's a gun to her head doesn't mean she's the one who pulled the trigger." He regretted it as soon as he said it. Sophia's eyes widened.

"You think she was killed?"

"We can't rule out the possibility yet." They stood there a moment, each caught in a web of dark thoughts. Dealing with a kidnapper was one thing. Dealing with a killer was another. "A cruiser is coming to take you back to Lisa's." She opened her mouth to complain but he kept on. "This isn't a discussion. If you want me to find your sister, you need to trust me. I have to do my job and this part will go faster with less people hanging around." He put his hand on her shoulder, hoping it provided some comfort. "I promised you I would find your sister and I will, okay?"

Sophia pursed her lips but nodded.

"And you'll call me as soon as you find something?" she asked.

"Of course." He dropped his hand from her shoulder. "I want you to call me or Tom if you need anything. Anything at all. Got it?"

She nodded again.

"And, Sophia? Do me a favor and lock the front door this time."

A CAVALRY OF PEOPLE showed up within the hour. The car and area around it had become a true crime scene buzzing with activity as everyone carried out specific jobs. Sophia was told to wait in the truck—away from all the action. She understood the delicacy that had to be taken with the body, fingerprints and any clues left behind, but that didn't stop her from feeling like an errant child told to go sit in time-out.

She wanted to help. Whether or not Trixie had killed herself or been killed, there were still two missing women out there and Sophia couldn't help but feel like time was running out.

She sighed—it almost felt painful. Her lack of patience was showing itself, though she doubted any normal person in her situation wouldn't be facing the same issues.

It was almost four in the morning by the time an officer came to collect Sophia. She wanted to stay and continue to watch Thatcher dissect the crime scene. The way he moved around it, the way his brow pulled together, the way his hands, now in gloves, moved across the surfaces of the scene, all had her enraptured. She had met men before who had taken their jobs seriously, but she had never seen Thatcher's kind of conviction in it. Then again, the men she was comparing him to had never had a dead body as part of their job description.

Officer Murphy, a man of few words, held the door open for her when she finally gave in—she couldn't deny the exhaustion that pushed against her body. Even an hour of sleep would be welcomed at this point.

Unlike the detectives or Officer Whitfield, the new cop was less than chatty on the ride to Lisa's. That was fine by her. They rode in silence for the fifteen-minute drive, giving her time to deal with the main reason she had broken down after seeing Trixie's body. If the second woman to go missing was already dead, then what chance did Lisa have?

It was a question that sliced through the hope she had been holding on to. The only reasons it hadn't completely disappeared was because of a tall man with dark hair and the most beautiful blue eyes. If anyone could find Lisa and Amanda, she had to believe it was Braydon Thatcher. Watching him work, his face set in unfailing concentration, Sophia knew he would keep his word. Or, at the very least, try with all that he had.

"This is it," Sophia told the officer as Lisa's house came into view. Instead of pulling into the driveway he parked in the road and opened the door. She threw him an inquisitive look.

"You stay here while I make sure the house is safe." He didn't give her any room to complain, a trait that most Culpepper cops seemed to have, and took her keys to go inside. He was out in less than five minutes with two thumbs up.

"Thanks," Sophia said, trying to keep her tone pleasant. Though her aggravation was tested at what he said next.

"Let me know if you need anything. I'll be out here in the car."

"You're staying?"

"Yes, ma'am."

"For how long?"

"Until I'm told to leave." He smiled and lifted his hands to stop her from responding. "Sorry, ma'am. Those are the orders."

Sophia didn't have the energy to protest. She thanked him for the ride and walked straight through the front door and didn't stop until she hit the bed. No guilt wound its way up as she sunk in between the loud, multicolored pillows.

For the first time in days no amount of worries could keep her awake.

SUNLIGHT FOUGHT ITS way through the blinds and lit the bedroom in a pleasant glow. When Sophia awoke she felt disoriented but oddly content. It was peaceful here. There were no car horns or sirens competing for airtime, just the buzz of the air conditioner and the soft hum of the ceiling fan. It was relaxing.

She rolled onto her back and stretched. Even though she had slept, there was still a blanket of exhaustion wrapped around her. The stress of everything didn't help. Sophia sat up and looked at her phone. It was barely nine on Friday, meaning she had slept for almost five hours. Guilt rose hot and fast at the realization. Were Lisa and Amanda able to sleep? Did their captor keep them awake, chained up to make sure they didn't escape? Were they even alive? She jumped out of bed, trying to erase the last thought. Feeling guilty wasn't going to help them.

Sophia took a quick shower to wake her up. The rest of the house may not have looked lived in but the bathroom was stocked with all the girly products she needed. Lisa had always been adamant about proper hair care.

When she finished she dressed in another pair of blue jeans, a gray T-shirt and tennis shoes. She didn't bother with makeup or working on her hair. Instead she flung it up into a ponytail, the ends dripping water onto the tile floor. However, she took a moment to spray some perfume on, unintentionally thinking of Thatcher as she did it.

He hadn't called or texted while she had been asleep. It concerned and annoyed her. Had they not found anything to use? Or had they found something that they didn't want to share with her?

The cop car was still sitting in front of the house. He *had* to know what was going on. She'd just have to get it out of him, a much easier task, she bet, if she had a peace offering. Though the pantry was almost empty, she spied a bag of blueberry muffin mix on the bottom shelf. The only ingredient they called for was water, taking twelve minutes to bake. Surely, the cop would be more willing to give her details while he munched on free breakfast.

Fifteen minutes later she was plating the delicious little confections when the doorbell rang. Her heart skipped a beat at the sound. She braced for bad news as she opened the door.

Sophia had never seen the man before. He was tall, fit and had a head full of dark red hair. He looked like the stereotypical Florida beach bum—a floral print button-down opened to show the white undershirt, navy swimming trunks, sandals and a pair of aviators over his eyes. He moved these up to the top of his head when the door opened, revealing eyes as black as coal.

"Hello," the man greeted, smiling wide. He outstretched his hand. "My name is Nathanial." On reflex she shook back. "You must be Lisa's sister, Sophia?"

"Correct..."

"I wanted to come by and give you this." He produced a handful of envelopes.

"What are these?"

"Lisa's mail from work. It was piling up and I knew some were payments for her services so I thought they'd be safer with you." She took them, looking over his shoulder at the stationary cop car as she did. Though she couldn't get a clear view of the officer's face, she could see his outline dutifully seated in the driver's seat. He must have known Nathanial to let him come up to the house.

"Thank you, I'm sure she'd appreciate it. Are you two friends?" Sophia's face heated slightly. She hadn't meant it to sound like that. She just didn't know much about the social circles Lisa had been running in the past year. Nathanial's name didn't sound familiar but, then again, neither had anyone else's minus Richard. "I'm sorry if that sounds rude, I just don't have the best memory when it comes to the names Lisa has told me."

"Oh, don't worry. We're more of acquaintances than friends. I work at Kincaid's Wood World next door to her office. We share a mailbox and I noticed her mail was piling up." His voice softened. "Have the cops made any headway?"

Sophia cocked her head to the side, confused. As far as she knew the general public had been left in the dark about the women's disappearances. Less panic meant more uninterrupted investigating. Nathanial caught on and explained before she could voice the question.

"This is a small town, Sophia. Word travels even when you don't want it to," he said with a sympathetic smile. She couldn't disagree with that.

"They may have found something this morning, so

we're hopeful about that." She decided gossiping to a stranger about Trixie's death wouldn't hurt anyone.

"I suppose all we can do is pray for the best." Sophia nodded. "Well, I'll leave you alone for now. Try not to worry too much, Sophia. It'll all work out in the end."

"Thank you, for these. *When* Lisa comes back I'll tell her you brought them."

Nathanial grinned. "That's the spirit."

She scanned each envelope to make sure there wasn't some kind of ransom letter or runaway note in the pile. Every piece had a return address. She dropped the mail on the counter, fully intending to sort through it later just in case. Privacy, be damned. She grabbed a plate of muffins for Officer Murphy. She would invite the officer inside if he told her what she wanted to know. If not, outside he would stay, she decided.

The Florida heat was back, making her regret the choice to wear jeans. The short walk across the yard to the cruiser was already activating her sweat glands. There was a forecast of potential rain later in the day, but that seemed like a long shot—there wasn't a cloud in the sky. For the past two days the only thing Culpepper seemed to revolve around was the shining sun, leaving sweat-inducing heat and hair-frizzing humidity. A drop in the temperature would be welcome at this point.

Officer Murphy had his head leaned back, eyes closed shut. She didn't blame him one bit. Watching a house would be boring to her, too, especially when operating on a lot less sleep. A part of her wanted to leave him be but a bigger part wanted some insider information.

"Officer Murphy?" Sophia knocked on the glass, the sound loud against the silence of the street. The man didn't budge. She knocked again. Nothing happened. He was really out cold, she thought with a smile. She wondered for a moment if she should give him some privacy and let the man sleep a little longer, but a quick gauge of her patience squashed that idea. She rapped against the glass once more before putting her hand on the door handle. "I'm going to open the door so please don't shoot me," she said more to herself than him. It wasn't locked, which she found odd. If you were trying to nap in a car, wouldn't you lock it? Especially if said car housed guns and the like? She pulled the door open wide and bent over a little to look at the man. He seemed peaceful enough— his face slack, head resting against the seat. "Officer Murphy?" she said gently, yet loud enough to actually wake him. The man remained as still as a statue. Sophia took a breath and prayed the man wouldn't shoot her. Being killed before Lisa was found just wasn't an option to her at this point. She moved a fraction closer and prodded his shoulder.

What had seemed like such an easy task—give a man some muffins in exchange for information—took a frightening turn. Around the man's neck were ugly red marks. Frozen, she looked at his chest, waiting for it to rise and fall. However, the only movement within the car was from her. Sophia's heart raced. With a shaky hand, she placed her fingers against the man's neck.

The plate of muffins crashed against the asphalt.

"Oh, my God."

Officer Murphy was dead.

Chapter Eight

This time Sophia had no problem locking herself in the bedroom. In fact, she ran there already dialing Detective Thatcher's number. All the while fighting the bizarre urge to clean up the broken dish left against the curb.

"Officer Murphy is dead!" she practically yelled when the detective answered. "I think someone strangled him! There are red marks around his neck and he isn't breathing!" There was no hesitation in Thatcher's reaction.

"Sophia, I want you to go lock yourself in the—"

"I'm already locked in the bedroom!" she said, cutting him off. "Officer Murphy is still in his car out front. I—I didn't know what to do with him."

"I want you to stay where you are and don't let anyone in or come out until I get there, you got that?" She chalked up his lack of surprise to his profession that called for calm and order in extreme situations. He was all business now. Normally, his orders would have rubbed against her stubborn side but she found herself agreeing adamantly. "I don't want to hang up but I need to make some calls. I'll be there before you know it. Call me if anything else happens."

He disconnected, leaving Sophia with her back against the wall, staring at the door. Someone had to be either incredibly stupid or incredibly reckless to kill a cop.

Whoever had killed Officer Murphy wouldn't bat an eye at killing her. Once they did that, there was no going back.

"Two dead bodies in one day," she mumbled. "I hate this town. I really do."

Sophia couldn't describe the relief she felt when sometime later she heard footsteps against the hardwood, followed by Detective Thatcher's voice. Belatedly she realized that in her rush to feel safe she had managed to skip the very important step of locking the front door. In hindsight it was a mistake that could have ended horribly but now all she could do was be thankful Thatcher was there.

"Sophia?" he called through the house.

"In here!" She undid the lock and opened the door wide.

"Are you okay?" There was no mistaking the worry in his voice. His eyes pierced into her as he closed the space between them. For a moment she thought he was going to embrace her—to fold her into his arms—but something stopped him. He took a slight step back. She tried to ignore the sting of the movement.

"I'm okay, just shaken up," she said, letting out a long breath, trying to calm down. "Did you see Officer Murphy? Is he really, you know, dead?"

He hung his head, a mixture of sadness and anger written plainly across his face. "Yes. Tom is out there with him. I need you to tell me what happened."

"Well, I hadn't heard from you when I woke up. I saw that he was still out there and thought that maybe he might know something. I was going to give him some muffins to try and loosen him up." She paused. It sounded silly when she said it out loud. "I went out there and thought he was asleep, but he just wouldn't wake up. I saw the red marks around his neck, felt for a pulse and freaked out. That's when I called you."

"You didn't see anyone or hear anything strange?"

"No, I woke up around ten then jumped in the shower. The only person I even talked to—" Her eyes widened. She had talked to someone. "There was a man who came by to drop off some of Lisa's work mail." Thatcher's body tensed so visibly she almost stopped talking. "He said he works at Kincaid's. You know, the wood shop next door to Details."

"Did he give a name?"

"Yes. It was Nathanial."

Thatcher grabbed her arm, a little too roughly.

"What did he look like?"

Sophia described the man, showing height and width with her hands. It was the second time the detective had an odd reaction to a piece of news. When she was done, he let go of her and took a few steps back. He ran a hand through his hair, his eyes wild.

"Do you know him?" she asked.

He didn't answer her but instead opened his cell phone to dial a number. "I want you to pack a bag," he ordered, the phone ringing.

"What? Why?"

"You aren't staying here anymore."

"Where are we—" He put the phone to his ear to cut her off.

"Go pack," he said with such resolution that Sophia didn't have the nerve to question him any further. He walked off as the person on the other end of the line answered. "It's Nathanial," she heard him say. "It's Nathanial. He's here in Culpepper."

That didn't sound good.

It wasn't a hard task to pack in a hurry—most of her

things were still in her bag. Thatcher's urgency had also lit a large fire under her bottom. She shoveled in her toiletries, plus a few she borrowed from Lisa's stash, and paused to look around the room. Sadness lurched across her heart. The death of Officer Murphy had, in a way, tainted the warmth of the house. His death felt like an omen—a great foreshadowing—of what was to come, though, Sophia hoped and prayed that the killing would cease.

The front door opened and closed, breaking through the dismal cloud that had spread around her. Without thinking, she grabbed the picture frame from Lisa's nightstand and put it in her bag. It was an old Polaroid of them as kids—a reminder of their bond before childish arguments had frayed it. With one last look at the brightly colored room and its equally loud pillows, Sophia turned off the light and started to go outside.

"How are you holding up?" Detective Langdon asked as soon as she cleared the door.

"I'm okay." The man patted her on the shoulder with a sympathetic smile. All in all Tom seemed to be a pleasant man. "I'm sorry about Officer Murphy."

"Thank you," he said, though his smile faded. "He was a good man. He was a friend." The moment could have turned into another wave of sadness but Tom soldiered on. "Where's the mail that Nathanial gave you?"

"On the counter. I glanced through the pile but didn't open anything. I'm sure my fingerprints are all over them, too."

"That's fine." He started to walk off but Sophia wanted an answer.

"Detective, it was Nathanial who killed Officer Murphy, wasn't it?" she asked, though she had already jumped to that conclusion herself based on Thatcher's reaction.

Tom didn't hesitate.

"We believe so."

Fear pulsed through her again.

"Then why didn't he kill me when he had the chance?" If Officer Murphy was already dead when he gave her the mail, then there was nothing stopping him from doing what he pleased. Why had she been spared when the cop was not?

"That's what we're wondering, too," he replied.

"Oh," she said, unsure how to respond.

"But we're glad you're okay," Tom tacked on. It made her smile but the expression didn't last.

"Tom, who is Nathanial?" Like Thatcher, his whole body visibly tensed. He looked at her with sympathy when he answered.

"Let Braydon tell you."

Tom ended the conversation without another comment and went to collect the mail. Sophia, having nothing more to do, settled into the front seat of Thatcher's truck.

Thatcher.

Sophia realized she had been referring to Braydon by his last name while she had no problem calling his partner by his first. It wasn't that she disliked the detective, in fact, it was the opposite that kept her from saying his name she realized. Somehow calling him Braydon felt more intimate and that was a feeling she needed to distance herself from. Thatcher was the detective on her sister's case. That was a fact she needed to respect, no matter how much the man intrigued her.

Two more cop cars and an ambulance showed up before he joined her. The sidewalks were filling up with Pebblebrook residents. Soon the gossip mill would be turning full circle, at its core Sophia and the deceased officer. One of the cops kept yelling at the bystanders to back up, but it wasn't hard to see that there was a body in the cruiser. Braydon kept quiet as he navigated around the ambulance and out of Pebblebrook. Sophia had so many questions. She didn't know which to ask first.

"What the hell is going on?" That would have to do for now. The direct question didn't unlock his lips. He was stuck on a cycle of checking his rearview mirror, a look of concentration on his face. "You're scared of him, aren't you? Nathanial."

This got a reaction. He laughed. It was unkind.

"I'm not afraid of that man," he said, slowing down for a stop sign. He met her gaze for a moment. "But I am afraid of what he'll do."

"He seemed nice enough when we talked."

"He was lying to you," he snapped.

"How do you know?"

"Because Nathanial has never worked a day in his life at Kincaid's. He also hasn't lived in Culpepper for almost eleven years."

"So you *do* know him."

"Yes," he admitted.

"But how? Who is he?" Sophia was tired of all the unknowns from the past few days. She wanted certainty. She wanted answers.

"It's a long story." He stalled. "Just know he's a—"

"No, sir!" she interrupted, raising her voice. "I don't want this runaround you're giving me. My sister has been missing for almost six days, I've barely slept during three of those and in the span of less than twelve hours I have seen two dead bodies. I'm not stupid, Detective. I know that finding Trixie, the second woman to go missing, doesn't bode well for Lisa. I'm trying to find hope here. So when I ask a legitimate question, I don't need you to patronize me just because 'it's a long story.' *You* need to tell me what's going on, starting with this Nathanial person." She could feel herself blush as she said it, but she meant each word, along with the heated persistence behind her appeal.

A silence filled the cab. It sent a chill down her spine.

"You're right." Thatcher's voice had softened. Another quiet settled—a bloated hesitation that hid an elusive truth. "You deserve to know, but before I tell you who he is, I need to tell you why he hates me."

BRAYDON DIDN'T WANT to tell this story. Hell, he didn't even like *thinking* about it. He could keep her in the dark if he wanted to, but if Nathanial was back, then he needed to tell her. She was now involved and he needed Sophia to understand the lengths that the man had already gone to and would attempt to go to ensure Braydon's misery. He needed to warn her to keep her safe.

"I was a bad teenager," he began, looking straight ahead. "I drank and partied, acted recklessly, stole, did drugs, and had a short fuse and a big temper. I was eighteen and thought I was invincible and no one could tell me differently. My parents tried, though. They tried to reach the sensible side of me, show me the error of my ways, but I was just a selfish kid. I didn't care about them or anyone else, except for one person. Her name was Amelia. She was my sister." He smiled. It was involuntary—a normal gesture that happened when he thought of his sister before the incident. "You talk about smart and beautiful with a good heart, that was Amelia. Though her jokes were lame." He laughed as he said it, lost in the feeling of remembering. "She never seemed to be able to say the punch line right. One time she—" He stopped, remembering the purpose behind the story. It wasn't a time to reminisce. He cleared his throat and continued.

"Amelia could have had any guy she wanted but decided to date Terrance Williams. They were together all of junior year and seemed happy enough but one day Amelia came to my room and said she didn't feel the same way about him anymore. She asked what she should do. I told her to break up with him—to end it. It didn't make sense for her to be with him and be unhappy."

He hit the steering wheel so hard it made her jump. "If I could take back that advice, if I could go back to that moment, I would."

"What happened?" Sophia asked. It was a gentle prod to keep the story going but was also laced with true curiosity.

"She ended it, but a few days later said they were going to meet up at what used to be 'their' spot. Just to talk, she assured me. I let her go with a nod and some teasing. An hour went by and I got a panicked call from Nathanial, Terrance's older brother on break from college. He said his parents found a suicide letter that Terrance had written and their handgun was gone. I told him where they'd gone and jumped in the truck and raced off to the Bartlebees' dock. Or, at least it was then. Now it belongs to the Alcasters. The Bartlebees traveled a lot so the kids used to use their dock to hang out around," he explained as an aside, remembering Sophia didn't know the local history. "I don't remember getting there but I do know I didn't once hit the brakes. I had the worst feeling sliding around my stomach—the feeling that something horrible had happened. I was right. I found Amelia's body there, two bullets in her chest." Braydon stopped, struggling with reliving the emotions. They dredged up anger so potent he could taste it. Sophia put her hand on his knee. The touch was enough to rein in the building rage and finish the story. "I looked around but couldn't find Terrance.

That's when I noticed the tire tracks. He had gone back to Dolphin Lot. I followed, ready to kill the little bastard, but he had already done it for me. Found him parked in the field, dead in the backseat with a gun to his head."

"Oh, my God, just like Trixie," Sophia realized.

"Turns out Nathanial was a few minutes behind me the whole time. He saw his brother just as the cops came in."

"So, what…he killed Trixie and set her up like that to send you a message? To taunt you?"

"Nathanial publicly blamed me and Amelia for everything. He said I had told Amelia that Terrance wasn't good enough for her and that Amelia had poisoned Terrance's mind, playing with it until he snapped. It was a big relief when the Williamses decided to leave town. Up until today, as far as I knew they haven't been back since." He sent her a significant look. "Other than the cops and coroner, Nathanial and I were the only ones who saw Terrance that day."

"So when you saw Trixie like that, you knew," she said, hand still on his knee. Its warmth could be felt through the material of his jeans.

"I wasn't a hundred percent sure that it was Nathanial. Everyone in town knows the story and he could have told someone all of the gritty details. I mean, I even entertained the thought that maybe the kidnapper put it together to throw me off—to bring up the past to try and confuse me, but then Nathanial showed up. It's all intended to be personal, I'm sure of that."

"You think he took Lisa and Amanda, too?"

"Yes. It would be too much of a coincidence if he didn't." He cast a worried look at Sophia. She took her hand off of his knee and placed it on her lap. There she began to wring them together in small circles. Braydon was coming to find out it was her nervous twitch.

"But why Lisa, Trixie and Amanda? What's the connection between them? And why did he talk to me? Why didn't he kill me like the officer?"

"Nathanial is a complicated man. Always has been. As of right now, I have no idea why he chose to take those women, kill a cop, yet not try anything with you. Maybe it was convenient, maybe it was random… Either way, I'll find out. We still don't know his endgame. I can only assume he just wants to show me who he is right now."

That's what worried Braydon the most. Setting up Trixie's body like Terrance's then talking to Sophia and killing the officer outside, these were the actions of a man who wanted his presence known. Why? It almost ensured he didn't have any place to run, to hide. Letting Braydon know who he was had effectively ended the man's normal life.

Why? Why now?

Sophia remained quiet. It was Braydon's turn to try to comfort her. He took her intertwined hands in his. There was a new feeling of guilt as her smooth skin pressed against his. Getting too close to her hadn't been his plan but he couldn't deny it seemed to be happening. Sophia was a part of the investigation. It wasn't professional of him to entertain a closer relationship than cop and civilian. It could endanger the case or, even more, his career. Yet, as he felt her hands in his, he pushed that guilt and worry out of his mind. He wanted to help her, to be there for her.

"Nathanial has a plan he's working through. Lisa and Amanda are still out there. We'll find them."

Sophia gave him a weak smile. He hoped he hadn't just lied to her.

Chapter Nine

Braydon drove to the police station, reasoning it was the safest place for Sophia while he worked. He hadn't said it out loud, but he was sure she was Nathanial's newest target. However, why he had taken Lisa and Amanda he could only guess. The Nathanial he had known before the incident had been a smart guy. This Nathanial was completely foreign to him.

The station felt like a modern-day tomb as they walked inside. All officers, minus the two assigned to stay, had been dispatched to Dolphin Lot and Lisa's house. No one would be getting speeding tickets today. The only other person left was the part-time receptionist named Lynda Meyer. She met them at the door with a flurry of blond curls and Press-On nails.

"Is it true, Braydon?" she asked. "Is James really dead?"

He nodded and a cry erupted from her throat. She threw her arms around Braydon for what she hoped would be a bonding hug. Braydon returned it, albeit awkwardly, before she let go and noticed that he wasn't alone. Her eyes turned into slits as she finally acknowledged Sophia. The blonde had been the most territorial woman he had ever dated, even if they had only gone on a handful of dates two years ago. She had more jealous bones in her body than probably even she knew what to do with. Braydon reached back and took Sophia's hand, showing Lynda that she needed to watch herself.

"Lynda, if you see Nathanial Williams at all I want you to lock the doors, grab a gun and call me immediately," Braydon instructed.

"Nathanial Williams…" Her eyes widened. "Is he the one who killed James?"

Braydon didn't answer but instead led Sophia through the door to the main room. Even with everything going on, he took small pleasure in how perfectly her hand seemed to fit in his.

"The conference room has a couch in it. You'll probably be the most comfortable in there." He ushered her into the room. The couch he referred to was a worn, uncomfortable piece of furniture that gave more neck and back cricks than anything the Culpepper PD had to offer, but Braydon didn't want Sophia sitting in his office. He didn't think Nathanial was stupid enough to walk into the station with a gun or a bomb, but, on the off chance he did, at least Sophia wouldn't be in the one room the crazed man would immediately search. Plus, he had to remember that this was the same man who just strangled a cop to death. "I need to go make some calls and I'll be back. The break room is the next room over and the bathrooms are off the hall that leads to the lobby." He dropped her hand, though he realized he didn't want to let it go, the heat their touch had generated leaving as they parted. "Will you be okay?"

Sophia nodded.

"I need to tell Richard what's going on," she said. Braydon was still unhappy with the rich man giving a stranger the key to Lisa's house, knowing Sophia was staying there, but he had to admit that same stranger had given them a big clue.

"That's a good idea. See if he's found anything." Like they all knew would happen, Richard's attorney had cleared the man with relative ease. He had returned to his house on Loop Road as far as Braydon knew. Unless the stranger and Richard's usefulness took a turn for the worse, Braydon might as well let him do what he was going to do anyway.

"On it." She took out her cell phone and sat at the conference table. He hadn't noticed until now how petite she looked not dressed in her power suit and heels. It was deceiving to think she was fragile. He was learning that Sophia Hardwick was anything but. She had been through a lot more than most and yet her head remained level, her resolve unbreakable. It alarmed him how much he wanted to protect her, to see her happy and to reunite her with her sister.

If Nathanial harmed Sophia in any way, Braydon would kill him.

THE CLOCK ON the wall was broken. It ticked with an uneven rhythm while the second hand was frozen over the six. For the past hour Sophia had begun to despise the clock and the stream of time it was tasked to track.

Sophia felt a stab of guilt in her stomach. She had been so wrapped up in worry for her sister that she hadn't given much thought to Trixie Martin's death. According to Thatcher, this woman had chosen to live a life away from normal social interaction. If it hadn't been for her boss, Cal Green, she may not have been flagged as missing for quite some time. The thought created a pocket of misery within her chest.

Did she have family or friends who would mourn her?

Surely, her boss and coworkers would? Had they already been notified? Sophia closed her eyes, overtaken with sadness. She hadn't thought about any of these things until now. What did that say about her character? The image of Trixie's lifeless body flashed behind her eyelids. Sophia shuddered. Her eyes flew open.

What about Amanda? Did she care about the other missing woman? It was a horrible question to ask herself but she knew it needed confronting. She was so determined to find Lisa that her concern for Amanda had been minimal. It put ice in her blood to realize it. *I do care,* she thought. *I just want my sister back. She's all I have.* The guilt that stabbed at her cut deeper.

"Knock, knock." Officer Whitfield stood in the doorway, a cup in each hand. She offered one to Sophia. "It's not the best brew in town but it'll keep you awake."

"Thanks." She was grateful for the warmth. It soothed the troubling doubts surrounding her quality of character. "I managed to sleep for a few hours but I still feel tired. This definitely helps."

"Can I join you?" Cara asked.

"Of course. It *is* your conference room, but I'd love the company." It was something Sophia didn't often confess but in the moment it rang true. She was dancing dangerously close to self-loathing while she was by herself.

Cara took the seat opposite and sipped at her coffee. Her eyes were red and puffy. She had been crying.

"I know you probably don't want to, but can you tell me what happened to Officer Murphy?" She looked sheepish, yet determined. "I've heard the condensed version but I need to hear what happened from you." There was a desperation there, underlined in shed tears and visible heartbreak. Officer Murphy had clearly meant something to her.

"Sure, I don't mind."

Sophia recounted everything that had happened from the time she began to bake to Nathanial's appearance to feeling for a pulse on Officer Murphy's neck to running inside. What Thatcher had told her about Nathanial on the car ride to the station only reinforced her past reasoning to flee the scene. Though, when she said it aloud, she felt that self-loathing again.

Cara was quiet when Sophia finished. She stared down into her coffee, a deep frown etched in her dark skin. Sophia wanted to comfort the woman but what could she say that would ease her sorrow? Officer Murphy had been found dead less than two hours ago. There was nothing she could say to Cara that could heal the pain. She instead gave her the silence she needed to sort through her thoughts. The clock ticked unevenly in the background.

"James was a good man," Cara finally said, her eyes beginning to water. "He was a damn good man." Sophia grabbed her purse and pulled out a pack of tissues. Cara didn't seem like the kind of woman who would appreciate being consoled with hugs and soft coos. She was like Sophia in that regard. Sometimes a person had to mourn alone for a while before she could mourn with others.

Sophia slid the pack across the table. Cara didn't look up as she took one and blotted at her eyes.

"He had a kid, you know?" A deep waver shook her voice as she spoke. "He's in fourth grade. James always was bragging on him, showing off his soccer trophies and honor roll ribbons. It got annoying after a while." She laughed. It was laced with tears. Grabbing another tissue, she wound it in between her hands.

"You two were close?" Sophia asked. She hoped it wasn't too much of an intrusion but the way Cara spoke seemed to tell two different stories. The cop nodded.

"When I first transferred here five years ago, I was the only female cop. Not saying that it was anyone here's fault, it's just that no woman had ever applied before. Most of the cops here now are good people but there are a few I could do without." She gave a weak smile. "When I first came in there were a few that didn't like that I was here. It didn't help that I was black, either. One night after my shift, I went home to find my house had been trashed. Windows broken, horrible things spray painted on the walls, my flower beds destroyed, and I won't even tell you what I found in the mailbox."

"That's horrible!" Sophia exclaimed. The woman waved off the concern.

"It's okay now, but back then I was devastated. It was clear that the people who did it wanted me gone but I didn't have enough money to leave. I also didn't have enough money to pay someone to help me repair everything. I remember sitting on my porch just crying my eyes out when a truck pulled up."

"James," Sophia guessed.

"Yeah. He got out and without saying anything he just started pulling out buckets, sponges, garbage bags and almost everything I needed to fix the house. When I told him I couldn't accept all that he had bought, he just smiled and told me I'd owe him one day. He came over after every shift and helped me repair everything. He wasn't the only one, Tom, Braydon and a few others helped, too, but it all started with James." She smiled. "We became close friends throughout the years."

There it was again, that feeling that the cop was leaving something unsaid. Sophia didn't question her this time. She didn't have to ask to understand that Cara had loved James. Had he realized? Did he love her, too? If

Sophia wanted to know, she was sure Cara wanted those answers with every fiber of her being.

She looked up to meet Sophia's gaze. There were tears and fire swirling in those brown eyes. "We'll find him, Sophia. We'll find Nathanial and make him pay for everything he's done. Braydon will see to that, especially since—" The cop caught herself. "There's history there," she amended, trying to keep Braydon's past personal.

"Braydon told me on the way here." There was no mistaking the surprise that jumped into the officer's eyes. She tried to hide it by blowing her nose again. Sophia took it that Braydon didn't often talk about his sister's murder. Not that she blamed him. If Lisa was killed, how would she handle it? That would be a bridge she would cross if the time came.

"I'm sorry about James," Sophia said, shaking herself. She had to keep hope that Lisa was still alive. That Nathanial was a man of theatrics with an unknown, devious plan and Lisa's turn in the spotlight hadn't yet come.

Cara wiped at a few tears that had escaped, then blew out a shaky breath. "Thank you." They fell into a silence that stretched between them, lost in their own thoughts, but connected by a common enemy. Nathanial could blame a lot of emotional trauma on the death of his little brother, of finding him in a field with a gun to his head, but he would never be able to justify the lives he had taken since.

Cara excused herself to the restroom, leaving Sophia alone once again with the unforgiving clock. After a few minutes of its broken ticking, she pulled out her phone and, for the first time in days, checked her email. Nothing new but advertisements and newsletters she had signed up for then promptly forgotten about. There were no messages from her boss, which made her nervous, though in comparison to everything that had happened so far it was almost silly to worry about job security. He'd given her "as much time as you need." She would have to take his word that her position as office manager would be waiting for her when all of this was over.

Thatcher won't be. She blushed at the unexpected thought. *He won't be waiting there for you. He'll be here.* The blush only seemed to deepen as the detective chose that moment to enter the room. The worry across his face hadn't ceased to exist—it was a constant mask he wore each time she saw him.

"I need your help." He handed her a large Ziploc bag with a thick, spiral notebook inside.

"This is Lisa's!" she cried, recognizing the blue book that rested inside. She'd given it to Lisa when she had started her business. It was jam-packed with sticky notes, magazine clippings, and had enough dog-eared pages to make a librarian cringe in disgust.

"We found this under the passenger seat of her car. I need you to look through it to see if you can find any information about who contacted her about going to Dolphin Lot and why. Also look to see if you can find a time that she went there. I would look through it myself but I figure you know her best and have a better chance of catching something I could miss. Plus, we're being stretched thin at the moment. We need all the help we can get." He ran a hand through his messy hair, only making it messier. She wondered briefly what it would feel like to run her hands through it. Would it be soft? Would it be coarse? If she pulled her hand away from it, would the smell of his shampoo linger across her fingertips? "We know *who* took them but we still need to figure out where. Maybe we can answer that by figuring out what happened at the beginning."

SOPHIA HAD FORGOTTEN how much of a scatterbrain her sister was until she was wrist-deep in the notebook. It seemed every idea she had ever produced had been transferred into the small pages in the form of sloppy notes, picture cutouts and the occasional doodle. Not only was the notebook filled with the aftermath of an ADD bomb, but it was also hard to navigate. For the first fifty pages or so, the notes were in chronological order. After that, as far as Sophia could tell, her brain had seemed to skip around, writing whatever she needed to in any space she could find. It was like looking into the mind of a hyper child. Sophia downed her coffee while trying to find reason within the chaos.

Thatcher had taken root at a desk closest to the conference room door, trying to figure out what Nathanial had been up to since he left Culpepper all those years ago. Cara had been ordered to go through all complaints filed in the past month from anyone and everyone in the hopes of finding one that involved Nathanial. Braydon believed that the man had been in town a lot longer than the past week. The crime scene on Dolphin Lot had been dissected and was still being processed, while a K-9 unit was searching the immediate area.

Sophia didn't know where Detective Langdon and the rest of the officers were at this point but she did know that Richard was at Lisa's house. When she had called him from the police station to update him on the situation he had already known what was going on.

"I'm well connected, Sophia. There's not much that goes on in this town that I don't know about." He had grown quiet for a moment. He didn't know where Lisa was, but she knew she didn't need to point that out. Braydon had come in then and spoken with the local tycoon. Richard had offered to stay in Lisa's house just in case

Nathanial decided to come back. He reasoned that the cops needed to be out in the streets looking for the mad-man instead of watching a house.

"Plus, I own several guns," he'd said.

When Braydon asked about the man with the missing tooth and his current whereabouts, Richard had admitted that the man had left town saying kidnappers he could deal with but killers was where he drew the line. Sophia guessed everyone, even those who tangoed with the line between legal and illegal dealings, had a limit and that had been his, though she was disappointed that there was one less person looking for the women. So there she sat, going through Lisa's almost hieroglyphic handwriting, trying to find a missing piece to the puzzle of what had happened Sunday.

"Any luck?" Cara asked after another chunk of time had slipped by. She had brewed a second pot of coffee and refilled Sophia's cup without asking. A gesture So-phia was grateful to receive.

"I can tell you what Lisa had for breakfast two weeks ago, I can tell you about the nightmare about clowns she had in April, I can tell you about the color scheme she's been playing with for a new marketing plan, I can tell you what kind of wedding dress she wants, and I can tell you, with certainty, that she hates counting calories." Sophia blew out a frustrated sigh. "But what I can't tell you is why she wrote down 'Dolphin Lot.' Why a twenty-nine-year-old woman can't seem to write in coherent sentences is beyond me." Cara reached over and patted the top of her hand. "What about you? Anything?"

She shook her head. "All the complaints filed have been small ones." She picked up the piece of paper closest to her. "Mrs. Miller called last week about the neighbor's dogs barking. A week before that it was Mike Anderson fussing about a rusty car that was parked outside of the Realtor's office." She lowered her voice. "He's a real stickler about keeping up good appearances." She put the paper down and took a gulp of coffee. "Other than that, there's not much in here, but I'll keep looking."

Sophia decided to take the break in work to ask something that had been in the back of her mind.

"Why are you being so nice to me?" she asked the officer without any relevant conversational segue.

"What do you mean?"

"Well, I understand being professionally polite but you seem to…I don't know…" She paused looking for wording that didn't make her sound rude. "You just have been genuinely nice to me and you don't even know me."

Cara didn't smile at first, which made Sophia afraid she'd offended her, but after a moment the officer's lips pulled up into a grin.

"You know that saying, 'Be kind, for everyone you meet is fighting a harder battle'? Well, I'd say you're in the middle of one of those." Her smile fell. "Plus, we're all in this together now."

The two women jumped back into their jobs, each digging for some kind of clue. Sophia looked up every so often to see Thatcher answering calls, pacing back and forth, talking to Tom and the captain who was now heading the Dolphin Lot investigation. When the phone calls were through he would sit back down at the computer, his fingers clicking away at the keys. It wasn't until three-thirty rolled around that he rose from his chair and came into the conference room.

"I think I know why Nathanial came back," he announced, leaning against the table. That grabbed Sophia's and Cara's attention. They looked at him expectantly. "I found a local news story from a paper in Arlington,

Texas, where a Lucille Williams overdosed on pills two months ago."

"Lucille Williams?"

"That's his mother. Apparently Dave Williams passed away five years ago, though I couldn't find the cause." He rubbed his eyes. It was the first time she noticed the matching baggage that hung beneath each.

"So, his mother supposedly kills herself and he snaps?" Sophia said.

"He wants someone to blame and picks the person he already holds responsible for his brother's death," Thatcher finished.

"Terrance kills himself and then his possibly still-grieving mother goes the same route. Two suicides in one family... That has to be hard," Sophia said.

"Tragedy isn't a free pass to do whatever you want, though," he added.

"True. Have you been able to track him? Do you know what he's been doing since her death?"

He shook his head. "That's the kicker. The last trace of him I could find was two years after he left Culpepper. He finished up his undergrad then disappeared. The only mention of him since then was the article about Lucille and it was just one line saying she was survived by her oldest son." He turned to Cara, sliding her a Post-it with a number and a name written down. "I need to run to the hospital to talk to the medical examiner about Trixie. That's the number of the newspaper that covered Lucille's death. I want you to talk to that reporter and find out if he knows anything about Nathanial." She nodded and left the room. Thatcher faced Sophia. His eyes softened, those pools of blue putting her at an ease she shouldn't have been able to obtain in this situation. "Stay here and keep working through that. If anything happens or you find anything—"

"I'll call you immediately," she finished with a smile. "I've proven that it's my first reaction anyway."

It was his turn to smile, though it only lasted an instant. "Be safe." With that, he was gone.

Chapter Ten

The Culpepper medical examiner confirmed what Braydon had already known—Trixie hadn't killed herself. In fact, like Officer Murphy, she had been strangled to death. The shot through her head had been postmortem, staged to get Braydon's attention and keep it.

"She was dehydrated but not starved. There's also no sign of sexual assault." She moved the sheet aside and brought Trixie's hand up to show him something.

"What am I looking at?" he asked, stepping closer.

"Nothing," she said.

He tilted his head. "I don't understand."

"That's the point," she said. "There is no dirt or cuts, no skin or blood under her fingernails."

"She didn't fight back," he filled in.

"I don't think she did, no." She put the woman's hand back down. "Did you know her, Detective?"

"I might have seen her once or twice at Green's but beyond that, no I didn't."

"I didn't know her all that well, either, but I did know she was an avid runner. I would see her running past my house occasionally. Her health before her death was impeccable—her muscles were strong."

"Then why didn't she fight back?" he questioned aloud. The ME snapped her fingers.

"That's what I wondered, too." She walked to the head of the table and uncovered Trixie's head. Braydon tried not to look too closely at her face, remembering the way Amelia looked when he had found her. She pointed to a red bump on the woman's neck.

"A mosquito bite?" It was a normal occurrence in the South. The little bloodsuckers fed off of the masses like a plague. "At first, that's what I thought, but I think it's an injection site."

Braydon's brow furrowed. He leaned closer to inspect it.

"You think he drugged her? With what? A tranquilizer?"

"I don't know yet but I sent the blood work out a few hours ago. I should hear something back by tonight," she said. "When I do, you'll be the first I call."

"Thanks." He stood straight, ready to leave when the ME sighed.

"It's sad, really. I saw her just last week running her little heart out."

Braydon nodded in sympathy when a thought occurred to him. "If you don't mind me asking, where do you live?"

"Sophia!" Cara yelled from outside the conference room. The sudden sound made her jump. She wasted no time in rushing out of the room.

"What? Are you okay?" She expected to see Nathanial standing in the room, ready to exact his wrongful revenge, but she was met with a giant smile from the female cop.

"He changed his name!" she exclaimed before turning to the computer.

"What?"

"I finally got a hold of the reporter who wrote that

story," she said, beginning to type. "I asked if he knew
Nathanial. At first he said no but then he told me that
he was threatened by the son to not include his name in
the article. So, I asked what *that* son's name was. You're
never going to guess what he said." She hit Enter and a
list of search results showed up in the browser. Sophia
came closer and gasped.

"Terrance."

"Yep. He took the name of his deceased little brother."
Cara whistled. "That's a special kind of creepy right
there."

Sophia had to agree. She looked at the list of articles.
The fourth from the top was an article congratulating
those awarded a Founder's Scholarship almost eight years
ago. Sophia took the mouse and clicked the link. The article popped up along with a picture of a group of college
students. Among them stood the younger Nathanial but
in the picture credit it said "Terrance Williams."

"It's almost brilliant if you think about it," Cara said.
"That's the one name we wouldn't have searched."

"Thatcher especially," Sophia agreed. It was an entirely different level of crazy. They took a moment to
read the article. Due to his high test scores and grades he
was being awarded a scholarship that would help pay for
the pharmaceutical engineering program he had just entered in New Jersey. The man may have had a few screws
loose, but Thatcher had been right—he was smart. This
fact did not help ease her worry.

Cara clicked out of the article and to the next one. "But
at least now we have a name to search."

Sophia went back to the little blue book while Cara
went to work putting together as much information
on Nathanial/Terrance as she could find. She flipped
through the pages again, having already looked at each

one. Her mind began to wander, despite her determination.

They were working under the assumption that Nathanial had snapped after his mother's death, but what if he had been crazy all along? Sure, it wasn't unheard of to name a child after a loved one, but to rename yourself? And only two years after the death? That kind of mind frame wasn't a stable one.

It made her wonder if he had changed his name as a misguided sentimental gesture or if it had been a part of a plan to drop off the grid—to hide from the eyes of cops almost nine years later. Was Nathanial's grudge that powerful or had it just worked out for him in the end?

She sighed. Her coffee was wearing off. The lack of caffeine wasn't helping the questions that buzzed around in her head like hundreds of angry bees. She took the pen she had been chewing on and started to doodle what they might look like. First, a big circle head with long hair and a stick body; second, the round insects with stingers and wings; third—

She stopped, remembering something she had seen in the middle of the notebook. Her heartbeat sped up as she flipped through pages. After a minute she found what she was looking for—Lisa had drawn a picture the size of a dime.

It was a dolphin.

Chapter Eleven

Lisa had always been horrible at Pictionary. Her drawing skills were less than desirable. Sophia had refused to be on her team whenever they were asked to play. It wasn't like she was much better, but Lisa couldn't draw any semblance of a circle and she even managed to mutilate stick figures. However, right then, Sophia could have kissed her sister's cheek.

The dolphin Lisa had drawn wasn't half-bad. Sure the fin was bumpy and the tail was crooked, but she was able to recognize it for what it was—an ugly, yet informative dolphin.

On top of the dolphin's head was a cone with wavy lines coming out the top. Sophia couldn't figure out what it was at first until she took another look at the dolphin's deformed tongue. It was a party hat, the tongue an uncoiled party horn that the dolphin was blowing out. Lisa had drawn one more addition to the festive creature— the number 630 on the edge of its fin, no doubt put there to look like it had a tattoo.

Lisa hadn't written out the message. She had drawn it.

She had gone to the Dolphin Lot at six-thirty in the morning to talk about a party.

It was her turn to yell out that she'd found a clue, just

as it was Cara's turn to jump in her chair. She showed the cop the drawing and watched as its meaning sunk in.

"Don't ask me why she couldn't have just written it out," Sophia said. "Just be thankful her drawing skills won this battle."

Sophia grabbed her cell phone and dialed Thatcher. She didn't know how the information would help but she was glad to announce she had found a clue. It brought her a sense of purpose, a sense of usefulness. She was helping find her sister, not just sitting on the sidelines wrapped up in self-pity.

"You okay?" he answered, worry thick in his voice. It made her blush, something she seemed to do a lot when involved with a certain detective.

"Yeah, I found something. Well, we both did. Can you talk?"

"Shoot."

Sophia told him about the dolphin and then about Nathanial's name change. Cara had already texted him about it but had compiled more information since. She handed over the phone and listened as the woman listed the highlights of "Terrance" Williams's past eleven years.

After Nathanial had left Culpepper, he went to finish the last two years of his bachelor's degree in chemical engineering. The name change came soon after and as Terrance he was accepted into a pharmaceutical engineering master's program in New Jersey. Two more years went by before he graduated with flying colors. Even as Terrance he disappeared for three years before showing up in a collegiate newspaper article as a source from a government research company called Microne, located in Texas. They specialized in running a national research lab, testing drugs created to target behavioral and mental disorders.

Sophia shook her head at that. It was like the pot calling the kettle black in a way. He was in charge of finding the right drug to help people who weren't stable. She had to wonder again if that had been the whole reason he had entered the field—to find something to water down his own crazy or if it was just a coincidence.

He showed up one last time before he was mentioned in his mother's overdose article. It was in a quarterly science publication less than a year ago. He had written a few paragraphs on his thoughts about sleeping disorders, but Cara admitted the words had been too big and she didn't understand any of what he'd said.

The cop quieted as Thatcher commented on the new information. Sophia felt like a child, suddenly annoyed that she wasn't in on the conversation. She had found a clue and now she wanted what? A pat on the head? A kiss from the detective? *I wouldn't mind that,* she thought with a quick smile. Cara passed the phone back, unaware of the odd grin, and began a new search in the browser.

"I'm on the way to Dolphin Lot right now," he started.

"Did the K-9 unit find something?" Hope and fear welled up inside. Hope that it was an even better clue to finding her sister, and fear that what they found *was* her sister.

"It looks like Nathanial had been camping out in the trees near Lisa's car."

"Why?" she asked, though didn't expect a completely sane answer at this point. The more she found out about Nathanial, the more unbalanced he seemed to be.

"My guess?" His voice stiffened. "He was waiting for me to find Trixie's body."

"That's starting to sound just like him," she admitted, feeling uneasy. "Do you think he was there when we found her?" There was a pause in which she imagined he shrugged.

"I don't know, but I'm hoping we can use whatever we find to track his location now. I'll give you a call if we find anything."

"Okay, be safe." It slipped out before she could stop it, but she truly meant it.

"You, too."

THE HEAT MIGHT have been bearable but the humidity was an altogether different story. It surrounded the men like invisible coffins—confining and inescapable. Braydon felt as though he was suffocating as he wove through the trees, following a cop from the county over. He didn't envy any of the officers' dark uniforms.

Captain Westin stood in a small clearing, looking like the only cop in Culpepper who wasn't sweating. A task Braydon attributed to the man's khaki shorts and white T-shirt. His badge hung on his belt and there was a cigarette lining his mouth. He looked like a regular Joe simply stopping in the woods for a smoke break.

"Captain," Braydon greeted. He had barely seen the man since Sophia had arrived. Westin grunted an acknowledgment and motioned to the scene around them.

There was a camping chair set up in the middle of the clearing. It was positioned so it faced out with a view unobstructed by trees, yet far enough away that it would be hard to make out a figure from where Lisa's car had been. A person would have to know exactly where to look and know what they were looking at to be able to see a man sitting there. Next to the chair sat a medium-size red cooler with its lid open. There was one unopened beer submerged in water. Empty beer bottles littered the area around both the chair and the clearing. Some were broken, lying at the base of a few trees.

"I'm guessin' he got bored waiting and did some target practice," the captain said, throwing an invisible bottle at the tree to their left.

"I'm just sorry it took me so long to find the car…and Trixie. He shouldn't have had time to get bored." The captain turned and clamped Braydon on his shoulder. The older man hadn't meant his comment to sound accusatory but Braydon still felt it. "The beer is local," he noted, looking at the Florida orange on the label. Only one place in town even sold it. He looked at the captain, comprehension dawning.

"Yep. I sent Tom out to get the security tapes from Tipsy's. I guess that's how he met Amanda Alcaster. Must have struck up a conversation with her while she was working behind the counter."

Braydon was getting ready to leave, blood pumping faster. He had finally gotten a break. "I'll go help him look through the footage."

"Not so fast, Thatcher." Braydon stopped in his tracks. "Sir?"

The captain took a drag of his cigarette and blew out a long stream of smoke.

"When's the last time you slept?" The question caught him off guard. His first reaction was to lie, knowing what would happen if he told the truth.

"Yesterday," he said. Westin gave him a look that said he knew that wasn't true.

"I want you to head home for a few hours and get some sleep. Tom and the rest of us can handle things in the meantime."

"But, Captain—"

"That's an order," he said sternly. "Just because Nathanial may want to play mind games with you, doesn't mean you're the only one who can take him down. This isn't a movie, son. Go get some sleep before you're useless to us."

Braydon knew better than to fight the issue with the captain. He also knew better than to attempt to sneak behind the man's back and continue working. On the way to his truck he called Tom and threatened that if he didn't keep him updated he would tell the entire force about Tom's want for Lynda. Once that can of worms was opened, there was no going back. His partner groaned but agreed to keep him in the loop.

The next call he made was to Sophia. He'd only known her for two days but it felt so natural to hear her voice.

"Do you want to sleep with me?" he asked after she answered the phone. He immediately slapped his forehead. Maybe he was more exhausted than he thought. "I mean, I'm being sent home to get a few hours of shut-eye and I figured you might want a place to crash, too."

There was a small delay before she answered. He knew she was going to do what he wanted to and complain that she didn't need sleep.

"We found a lead in the clearing. It'll take a little bit to sort through but Tom and the captain are on it. They promised to let me know as soon as they have anything." He could still feel her hesitation. "If we don't get some sleep we're useless, Sophia. They are good, smart men. They'll more than make up for our absences for a few hours." He had basically regurgitated what he had just been told but, he had to admit, it was reasonable. Sophia relented.

"I'll be there to get you in fifteen minutes."

They hung up and Braydon was left in the silence of the cab. It had been one hell of a week. He could feel it in his bones. He resisted the urge to check the mirror to see how many gray hairs had sprouted since he learned that Lisa, Amanda and Trixie had gone missing. It seemed like years had passed since Tom had joked about the job of detective being boring. Now Braydon wished he could claim such a thing.

Never would he have thought the young man he had known so little of in his youth would turn out to be a psychotic killer—an apparently *brilliant* psychotic killer. He imagined himself as a comic book character, constantly trying to battle evil while Nathanial was his nemesis whose life's mission was to ensure the destruction of the hero. Not that Braydon thought he was the hero. He was just a man with a new job, people counting on him and a madman to stop. Like the captain said, just because Nathanial had focused his sights on Braydon didn't mean they were alone on the playing field.

The detective's thoughts slid over to the glossy-haired, green-eyed, feisty Sophia Hardwick. She was a bomb in a sexy, stubborn shell. Most of the women he knew would have stayed at home and let the cops deal with the investigation or, if they wanted to help, they would stop at the word *no*. Not Sophia. In a way she reminded him of his sister, Amelia. When she had her mind set on something she went for it full tilt, not once stopping to question herself. Braydon's mother, while in a cloud of grief, had said that it was that specific quality that had been Amelia's undoing, but he had disagreed and he still did now. Her undoing had been a seventeen-year-old, mentally unstable boy and the handgun his parents kept around for safety.

Wondering about Terrance's sanity led him to the subject of Nathanial's. What Officer Whitfield had found was yet another reason to be extremely worried about the man's stability. Every time they learned something new about Nathanial, Braydon's concern for the safety of Lisa, Amanda and Sophia intensified.

He ran a hand down his face as he pulled up to the station. He may not have killed Trixie or James with his bare hands, but he was the reason they were dead. The kidnappings, too, were just Nathanial's scheme to punish his mortal enemy. If anything happened to Sophia... He punched the steering wheel.

He wasn't going to let anything happen.

Chapter Twelve

Braydon lived in a small, traditional two-bedroom, one-bathroom house in the middle of Gothic Street. Though the name inspired dark images, most of the houses sported a variation of tan, beige, yellow and orange siding. His was a rich cream color with a blue front door and a large wooden front porch. That front space had sealed the deal the moment he saw the house.

The house at 2416 Gothic Street was the first and only property Braydon had ever purchased alone. It might not have been the biggest house but it had hardwoods throughout, nice butcher-block counters, and a backyard that was big enough for a Great Dane. He was proud to call it home, and he couldn't deny it felt good to see it. Inside he pictured his king-size bed that barely fit the room, the tall shower that he no doubt needed after such a humid day and the refrigerator that was full of food. He sighed. The last time he had been grocery shopping was the week before; aside from a bag of chips and canned vegetables, the food selection was slim.

"This is nice," Sophia said as the truck came to a stop in the driveway. "I like the porch." Braydon smiled a genuine smile.

When they got inside he gave her the grand tour, which wasn't much. The front door started a hallway that led to the back door and screened-in porch, splitting the living room to the right and the kitchen to the left. Behind the kitchen was the bedroom that stood opposite the bathroom and guest room that doubled as his office. She was politely interested as he pointed out each room and once she even complimented his taste. He knew it was her reaching for a generic compliment—his decor was wood on wood on wood with two leather couches thrown in. He was what some people would refer to as "married to the job." When he had time off, he had higher priorities than decorating.

"Make yourself at home," he said, walking to the kitchen. He opened the refrigerator to confirm its near emptiness. Sophia peeked around his side.

"Looks like you don't cook much," she said. "I guess you go out a lot?" It sounded like an innocent question but Braydon had a feeling it was pointed. Sophia wasn't meeting his gaze. He realized with a smile that, while he knew she was romantically unattached, the subject of his dating life hadn't been discussed in detail. All she knew was that he wasn't married.

"I admit, I'm a big fan of takeout." He shut the door. "Looks like it's time to order some now."

"Hold that thought." Sophia walked to the open pantry and picked up the bread. She checked the expiration date, nodded when it was okay and went back to the refrigerator, taking out the lone pack of cheese. When she made sure it was good to eat, too, she held up both in victory. "How do you feel about grilled cheese sandwiches?"

"Marry me," he said, taking the hand that held the cheese. It was supposed to be a humorous gesture but as soon as their skin touched, he knew neither of them were thinking about sandwiches. The kitchen became heated. It felt exceedingly smaller and much more quiet than it was seconds before the contact. Her hand, soft and warm, was cradled in his own large, slightly calloused hands. They fit together like two puzzle pieces. Braydon looked down at them, convinced the warmth he felt was a moving, tangible entity.

Sophia returned the gaze, her head tilted up a few breaths away from his lips. He could do it. He could kiss her, let her know that what he felt for her had changed and was still changing. Her sage-green eyes were wide yet soft.

"So I take it you like grilled cheese?" There was an undercurrent to her question. He didn't let go of her hand.

"It's grown on me," he answered, wondering if they were even talking about sandwiches anymore.

A small smile started to form across her red lips. Braydon wondered if the color was lipstick or natural. He wondered what they felt like, too.

Why not find out?

SOPHIA HELD THE BREAD and cheese as if they were life preservers and she was a drowning swimmer. Which wasn't too far off in her mind. This was uncharted territory she was sailing. The desire she felt for the detective had seemingly come out of nowhere. True, it had been two days since she had met the man, but that still didn't discount the way she felt.

On the outside it must have looked odd—the two of them standing there, her hand and cheese clasped in his, but she didn't care. She was mesmerized. Raising her chin a fraction, she was able to get a better view of those calming aquamarine eyes. Something inside her ached as he searched her face. She wondered distractedly what it was. She decided that it didn't matter. Her feelings were turning out to be just as mysterious. She definitely couldn't ignore them, either. There was the possibility that their chemistry was a result of their heightened emotional states and desperation to find the missing women. However, there was also the chance that Braydon Thatcher could be the answer to a question her heart needed to know, and, if he wasn't, she could at least give the man a trial run.

Sophia had spent the better part of the past four years trying to climb the career ladder through Jones Office Supply, starting as low as an unpaid intern. She had liked the stability the job had offered and her focus had been on building a financial foundation and not much else. She had been friendly and had socialized regularly, but nothing had seemed to stick. Acquaintances became friends but not close ones. Once she fell into the sad loop of leaving work to go home to an empty apartment, it was hard to break. She hadn't purposely secluded herself, she had just worked long, unnecessary hours in an attempt to get that heavenly raise or the ever-elusive promotion. It hadn't bothered her then, but being with Thatcher, smelling his cologne, feeling the heat radiate off his skin, imagining what his body felt like against hers, she realized there was a hole inside her. It had been empty for years.

Overcome with a longing that raced from the top of her head to the tips of her toes, Sophia pushed up on her heels and kissed the detective full on the lips. She believed she was a proactive sort of woman—if she wanted something she went for it—but kissing Braydon Thatcher had been impulsive and an action she hadn't intended to take when they first entered the kitchen.

At first it was just Sophia's lips pressing hungrily against his, marveling at the rough skin. Then, after a moment, he returned the kiss with a slow deliberation.

Sophia felt a thrill of pleasure as their lips moved in tandem, unveiling a common desire. It may have started off slow but that wasn't the case for long. It picked up speed and momentum. All of the desperation, anxiety and fear that the past few days had brought had evolved into a single need for each other. A need that burned red hot between their lips. In that moment Thatcher became Braydon in her mind.

Braydon didn't drop Sophia's hand after the change in action started. Instead he used the grip to bring her closer into his chest while his other hand wound to the back of her neck and knotted in her hair. His tongue parted her lips and invaded her mouth with his intoxicating taste. Sophia wanted him closer still. She moved her free hand up his back and around his neck, becoming her anchor in the sea of uncertainty that was the town of Culpepper.

There they stood, intertwined in the kitchen, moaning against each other's lips, all thoughts of the world around them falling away.

Bliss, as Sophia had learned at any early age, didn't last forever. Their kiss was interrupted by the loud buzz of Braydon's phone pulling them out of the moment like a gunshot in the empty house. He dropped her hand just as she released him, though she didn't want to, and stood back in anticipation. If there was a lead in the case, they needed to know and they needed to know right then.

"Braydon here." His voice was filled with grit, his lips a dark red. Sophia couldn't hear what the female voice on the other end was saying. Judging by his calm facial expression, she assumed it wasn't the call that said they had found Lisa, Amanda or Nathanial. Braydon lowered the phone. "Officer Whitfield found out some more information on Nathanial. Give me a sec."

Braydon took the rest of the call in his office while

Sophia took a minute to try and cool down from the heated exchange. It wasn't as if she had never been kissed before. She'd been kissed enough. However, kissing Braydon had stirred up a new feeling inside. One she hadn't expected lived there, but one she definitely wanted to explore. It wasn't until her stomach growled loudly at her that she decided food was important. She searched the kitchen for a pan and began to make what she believed was one of the detective's favorite foods while her body rode out the remaining highs of passion.

It had been a long while since she'd been with a man and that relationship had just been overshadowed by a minute of kissing Braydon Thatcher. She put her fingertips against her lips. They were tingling with excitement. She could still feel him against her. It was a foreign yet familiar feeling.

Sophia smiled to herself as she cooked alone in the kitchen. Not only had she kissed him, but he had also kissed back.

"I'm going to jump into the shower real quick," Braydon said when he came back into the kitchen. His face was drawn, a frown living where his smile had been. It pushed the remaining thoughts of being wrapped in his embrace away.

"What did Cara have to say?"

"Nothing that leads us to him yet, but enough to make everything more complicated." He sighed. "Let me take a shower, then I'll catch you up. Deal?"

Sophia nodded. The moment between them was gone, replaced by overwhelming concern for Nathanial's victims. They didn't have time for a kiss to become anything more. They needed to stay focused. Though, Sophia wondered what that "more" would be like.

Braydon came back smelling of men's soap and wearing a white undershirt and a slick pair of gym shorts. He certainly looked more comfortable than he had before.

"Sorry, I needed a shower really badly," he said, looking sheepish. "I haven't been home in almost three days."

"You could have fooled me," she said with a wink, the aftermath of the kiss making her feel more comfortable with flirting with him. He laughed and sat down at the small, round dining room table. It sat four but with their plates and cups on top, only two could fit comfortably. Sophia bit into her grilled cheese while Braydon started.

"Nathanial was fired from Microne a month after his mother killed herself. He had been caught doing unauthorized testing on a new product for people suffering from severe sleeping disorders brought on by high levels of anxiety and stress."

"Unauthorized testing?"

"He apparently thought it was a good idea to take it home and use it on himself, which, I don't have to tell you, is a big no-no," Braydon said. "Cara talked to a former member of his research team who described Nathanial as meticulous and almost obsessive when it came to this specific drug."

"What was the drug?"

"They couldn't tell us because it's still in the first stages of testing. Which is another reason Nathanial got the boot. Human trials were at least a year away, if not more."

Sophia took another bite of her sandwich, absorbing this new information.

"Let me tell you why this information is a little more interesting to me," Braydon said. "Trixie Martin didn't put up a fight when she was strangled, or at least as far as the medical examiner can tell. Trixie is a strong woman so the ME suspected she was drugged." Sophia's eyes widened and her mouth gaped. "There was a welt on her neck with a tiny hole in the middle."

"Like from a needle?"

He nodded. "The ME sent off the blood work to confirm if it was or wasn't a drug that kept Trixie from fighting."

Sophia rubbed her neck, subconsciously thinking of Trixie being strangled. Officer Murphy had met with the same fate. Did that mean he would do it to Lisa and Amanda, as well?

"Was there anything else the medical examiner found that could be useful?"

"Only that she was strangled around Monday morning and the gunshot was postmortem. Everything else is just speculation at this point. I also think that she was killed there in the field."

"But her boss said she hadn't been to work in two days, right? She couldn't have been killed Monday," Sophia said, not understanding.

"Cal confirmed that Monday was her day off. She lives alone and keeps to herself so no one knew that she was even missing then."

"But what was she even doing there? Why did Lisa go to the lot on Sunday, then Trixie on Monday?" Sophia blew out a frustrated sigh. Braydon put down his sandwich and held up his index finger.

"I might have the answer to why Trixie was there." He left the room. Sophia finished off her sandwich with interest.

"This is a map of Culpepper," he said, coming back with a pocket-size road map. He put it on the table. "This is where Trixie's house is." He pointed it out with one index finger. "And this is where Dolphin Lot is located." He placed his other index finger on it. "It's roughly 10.5 miles apart." The detective slid his fingers across the space until they touched. Sophia still didn't understand. She shrugged and cast him a look that said "So?"

"Trixie was big on running. When we searched her house there were runner's medals and trophies everywhere. A lot of those were for marathons and triathlons. The medical examiner said she saw Trixie run by her house almost every day for part of training." He pointed to an area that was within the 10.5 distance between Trixie's and Dolphin Lot. "I think the Dolphin Lot road was part of Trixie's running route."

Sophia was alarmed. "But that's a twenty-one-mile run!" she exclaimed.

"Marathons are around twenty-six. Twenty-one miles wouldn't be unheard-of for her."

She sat up straighter in her chair. "Okay, so she goes for a run and then what? She sees something she isn't supposed to? Then he gives her some kind of weird 'pass out in a hurry' drug and then kills her before staging her death just like his brother's?" As she said it out loud, she felt a chill run up her spine. Braydon nodded.

"I think that's exactly what happened to her. I think she was running that route and maybe saw Lisa's car or Nathanial. In his sick mind he saw it as an opportunity he couldn't pass up."

"But why did Lisa go to the lot? I mean, I get it was about a party but who called it in? Nathanial? Was Amanda there, too?" There were too many questions surrounding Dolphin Lot. Why hadn't Lisa told Richard or called Sophia to tell either of them where she was heading?

"We'll find out." He clasped his hand over hers and gave it a squeeze. Unlike the electricity of the kiss, his touch held a blanket of comfort. "We found some good evidence in the woods on Dolphin Lot. I'm hoping it can give us some new information to follow." He proceeded to tell her about the clearing and its creepy contents, including the mass amount of local beer bottles. He put his full confidence in Tom and the captain to sort out the videotapes from Tipsy's and connect a few dots while Braydon took a much needed break. The news brought forth more hope than she'd had in the past twenty-four hours.

"Did Cara figure out where Nathanial went next? After he was fired from Microne?" Sophia wanted to know as she cleaned up the empty dishes. Braydon patted his nonexistent gut, appreciative of the power of a good grilled cheese.

"We still aren't sure. We checked with the apartment he lived in since he got the job there but he got out of the lease just after he was fired. They have no idea where he went. No forwarding addresses or a valid phone number to reach. He fell off the radar."

"That's not disturbing or anything," she said sarcastically. "Does he have any more family?"

"No, ma'am. His mother was the last bit of his family."

Sophia didn't want to empathize with the insane man, but she could do it. If she lost Lisa she would have no more living relatives that she was connected with. She would also lose her closest friend. It was a thought that wasn't fun to entertain but had to be downright horrible to live through. Although, it didn't excuse going on a killing and kidnapping rampage.

The kitchen quieted. Sophia rinsed the dishes off while Braydon pulled something from the freezer. A grin broke out across his face.

"I may not have all of the necessities but you have to give me credit for this." He held up a carton of chocolate ice cream. Suddenly, he was more attractive than ever.

They settled back around the table with bowls filled with frozen deliciousness. Sophia could pretend to have self-control all she wanted, but put some chocolate ice cream in front of her and it was game over. She attacked the sweet goodness with speed and vigor.

"So, if you don't mind my asking, what happened to your parents? I haven't heard you really bring them up."

Braydon waved off her discomfort. He didn't mind her asking.

"Oh, they're alive and well. Living in Utah near my father's relatives. They moved to Culpepper after they married, following my dad's job at the automotive plant that used to be downtown. They used to love it here but after Amelia died they moved. They said they couldn't stand to live in a place where their daughter was killed." He was so candid about it. Sophia wondered if it was easier that way—to state is as a fact.

"What about you?" she asked, sincere. "Why didn't you leave, too?"

"The reason why they left was the same reason I had to stay." He shrugged nonchalantly. "This town was the last place Amelia was alive," he said. "I left once and considered never coming back, but no matter how much pain I felt in Culpepper, the good memories outweighed it. Where my parents saw reminders of Amelia's death, I saw reminders of her life." His lips turned up in a small smile. "We grew up here so when I'm feeling low and want to remember the good times with her, I have an entire town to help me. I can go to the park and see her playing there when she was younger, the high school stadium where I'd take her to games when she managed to bug me enough for a ride, Jefferson Road where she tried to learn to drive and took out Mr. Jensen's mailbox." He let out a breath and licked his spoon. The small smile was still attached. In that moment he seemed years younger—no lives on the line, no killer on the loose, no worries. She quite liked it on him. "It's true, these memories can sometimes be depressing but they also do the soul good. I could leave Culpepper if I had to, but it's because of these memories that I don't want to." He pushed the last bit of ice cream into his mouth. His eyes shone bright as he met Sophia's gaze.

"That's a beautiful way to remember her," she said. He smiled for a second before his face darkened like a storm surging through blue skies.

"Nathanial hates me because he knows that I would have killed his brother had Terrance not done it first. Not only would I have killed him, I would have made him suffer. I *needed* him to suffer—to pay for what he had done—and I didn't care what that meant for my future." Braydon grabbed her hand across the table again, urging her to pay attention to what he said next. "That's how I know that Nathanial won't stop. Not until he knows I've suffered. I don't think he's dangerous, Sophia. I *know* he is. I'm sorry for all that's happened. If it wasn't for me, then Lisa and the others wouldn't have been taken."

He tried to let go of her hand but she held firm.

"Braydon, I'm only going to tell you this once. I don't and will not blame you for the actions of a psychotic man. You did *nothing* wrong."

"But now I'm afraid he's after you." She may not have known Braydon as long as his partner or even Lynda, his ex—according to a conversation she'd had with Cara earlier—but she did know that the vulnerability he was showing now was rare. It pulled at her heartstrings.

"We don't know that for certain," she said.

"He wants to make me suffer. What better way than to use you?"

"You care about this entire town and all of its people. He can use any of us." She said it to lighten the mood. They were skating around saying something significant again. Sophia could feel it. She watched as the conflicted man next to her chose his words carefully.

"He knows you're different."

Sophia's stomach fluttered with pleasure as if she was in high school again. Braydon, however, was still frowning. This wasn't the time for another moment between them. The burden he believed he placed on her seemed to be crushing him.

"What makes you think Nathanial going after me has anything to do with you? Have you seen me smile? I'm just too adorable," she joked. He looked as though he was going to argue with her but stopped short as she grinned wide, showing teeth and gums. Braydon squeezed her hand and the corner of his mouth quirked up. "Now, if you don't try to get some sleep I'm going to tell the captain on you."

He let out a loud breath, exaggerating his feigned annoyance. "Fine. I guess a few hours might do the brain some good." They parted hands and stood. "It wouldn't hurt you to catch some shut-eye, too. You can sleep in my room. I threw on some clean sheets when I got out of the shower."

"Where will you sleep?"

Braydon laughed. "Don't worry, I'll be out here on the couch." Sophia hadn't been worried. She could share the bed with the detective, though if they did that sleep may not be what happened.

"You don't have to do that. I don't mind taking the couch," she said instead.

"I'd feel more comfortable staying out here." He motioned to the front door and then the back. "If anyone tries to get in, I'll be the first to see it."

"Ah, Detective Watchdog." She smiled.

"That's my job. If you need anything you know where I'll be."

They said their good-nights and Sophia headed back to the bedroom. She hadn't noticed how heavy the bags beneath the detective's eyes had been but she suspected that as soon as he put his messy head of hair down he would immediately fall sleep. She switched out her outfit for a matching tank top and shorts combination, wishing for an instant it was sexier, and slid under the cotton covers.

The next day would mark the seventh day that Lisa had been missing. Seven days with the off-balanced, vengeful Nathanial Williams. If she ever saw that man again, Sophia didn't know what she would do but she knew it wouldn't be good. He may have lived through the tragedy of Terrance dying, then the passing of his parents, but punishing Braydon and killing and kidnapping wasn't the answer. He had lost his sanity. The time for intensive therapy or religious salvation had passed. He had condemned himself the moment he decided vengeance was the answer.

She crawled farther under the covers and inhaled deeply. Braydon's scent surrounded her, clinging to the cotton she was nuzzled in. If someone were to tell her she would be in Detective Thatcher's bed when she first came to town, she would have laughed in their face. Her affection for the man had snuck up on her through the course of the investigation. He was strong, determined and wholly committed. The way he had kissed her tonight…it sent a thrill across her body and soul. She imagined how it would feel to press her lips against his again, to run her hands through his dark hair, to feel the warmth of his embrace, to lose herself completely in him.

It was enough to temporarily ease the emotional turbulence over Nathanial Williams.

Sophia bolted awake, terrified and disoriented. *This isn't my bedroom,* she thought. *This isn't Lisa's bedroom, either.* She looked around the dark space with wide eyes trying to figure out where she was and what had woken her. The dresser opposite the bed had a pair of men's jeans folded on top. *I'm at Braydon's.* She remembered. *But what woke me up?* Sitting still, she listened.

There was a faint noise that was coming from the living room. It came in rhythmic bursts but she couldn't quite place it. Pushing her legs over the bed, she crept across the wood floors and opened the door slowly.

The mystery sound belonged to Braydon. He apparently was a man who snored quite heavily. She tiptoed toward the living room and looked at the prone man.

"Oh, my." She said out loud before slapping a hand over her mouth. Braydon had shed his shirt and shorts after she had gone to bed. Now she had an uninhibited view of a rock-hard six-pack with a smattering of dark hair that led from his pecs down to a region the blanket just barely covered. There were muscles everywhere, it seemed. She stood there looking at them, bathing in all of their sexy glory. *And to think, I was kissing that earlier.*

Feeling as if she was getting close to being creepy, Sophia turned to retreat back into the bedroom when a loud *thump* stopped her. She froze in the hallway. Then the sound of a car door slammed. She turned and walked to the front window, moving the curtain to the side. The road outside was void of people and cars but there was a large lump on the front porch. With dread filling her veins, Sophia turned on the light.

"Braydon!" she yelled before opening the front door. Behind her she could hear the man jump up. She was already on the porch when she called for him again. "Braydon!" She dropped to the ground next to the body. Fear cascaded down every inch of her, pooling along with the blood that surrounded the woman. Immediately Sophia knew it wasn't Lisa. This woman was too short. A small ounce of relief sprouted. "Braydon!" she yelled again.

Braydon ran through the living room to the front door, bare feet slapping against the hardwood. The man always came to her when she called, but this time it wasn't her who needed him. He flung the screen door wide.

"What the—"

"I think it's Amanda." Sophia moved the woman's long hair aside to feel for a pulse. She ignored her shaking hand as she felt a faint beat. "She's still alive!"

Braydon ran back inside to grab his phone. He was back in a flash, phone to his ear.

"Find out where she's bleeding from," Braydon commanded. "We need to see if we can stop it." Sophia looked down at the woman resting on her stomach. Her cheek was pressed against the wood of the porch, eyes shut and lips downturned. In the poor light of the porch's singular bulb, Amanda looked unnaturally pale. Sophia surveyed her back and legs but couldn't find the source of all of the blood.

"Help me turn her over." Braydon put the phone on speaker and told the operator his address while they grabbed Amanda and flipped her over as gently as they could. Blood had soaked into the front of her shirt yet there were no holes or tears in the fabric. Sophia grabbed the hem of the shirt and pushed it up. The source of the crimson made her gasp.

Braydon swore. He finished up with the operator and ran inside to grab a towel. "We need to stop the blood flow!" he yelled back.

Sophia's body had gone numb. She couldn't believe her eyes. Carved into Amanda's stomach was her name.

Chapter Thirteen

The Culpepper hospital was a twenty-minute drive across town. Sophia rode it in the back of an ambulance while Braydon sped behind. If there were any doubts of Nathanial's intentions to use Sophia against the detective, they were gone now. Even Sophia couldn't deny that the crazed man had targeted her. After Braydon had returned with the towel he gave Sophia his gun and all but pushed her inside. There she had waited until the sirens came closer.

Braydon was so visibly shaken and equally on alert that Sophia was surprised she had been able to talk him into letting her ride in the back of the ambulance at all, but there had been no way she was going to let the poor woman ride alone. Plus, if she woke up, Sophia *had* to ask the one question that had burned inside her chest since she had come to town. Where was Lisa?

However, Amanda didn't wake up. The EMTs bustled around her, strapping an IV on and checking her vitals. They didn't talk to Sophia the entire ride, but after they saw her name carved into the young woman's flesh, they couldn't keep their eyes off her. She didn't blame them one bit.

In the back of the ambulance, Amanda looked a lot worse. Her clothes, a band T and cargo shorts, were fully intact but covered in blood and dirt. Her feet were bare and stained with a mixture of red and brown while her hair looked as though it was wet with sweat or grease. The pulse Sophia had felt was weak and, as one of the EMTs said, Amanda had lost a lot of blood. Seeing her lying on the stretcher, body sliced and bleeding, Sophia hoped that Amanda had at least been unconscious when Nathanial decided to brand her stomach.

When the back doors of the ambulance opened, Braydon's face was the first that swam into view. He helped lower Amanda's stretcher down and ran alongside her, telling the nurses inside the situation. Sophia ran behind them, keeping out of the way but just within earshot. A doctor came out, evaluated Amanda and told an orderly to start prepping a room for surgery. Apparently her condition was worse than Sophia had thought.

"He cut her too deep," Braydon said after the chaos had died down a fraction and the woman was being taken into surgery. He gave Sophia a significant look. "There was a bump on her neck."

"From the drug," she stated. Instead of nodding he threw his fist into the wall of the waiting room. A few nurses eyed him warily before turning back to their jobs. Sophia reached out and grabbed the fist. He met her eyes, the fire in them almost burning her.

"I'm going to make him pay," he said. "You just wait."

Sophia couldn't blame him for the reaction. Now Lisa was alone with the man, if she was even still alive.

"So what now?"

Braydon ran a hand through his hair. At least the bags under his eyes had lessened with the few hours of sleep they were able to get.

"Amanda is going into surgery in the next twenty minutes. There was a welt on the back of her neck, so I told them about the drug we suspected she was injected with. They are trying to figure out what it is before they put her under. If they can't, then it could kill her." His frown deepened. "I called the captain and Tom on the way here. They'll look for him while an officer stays with the surveillance tapes. I also called Marina Alcaster. She needs to be here just in case Amanda doesn't make it, so she can, I don't know, see her daughter alive once more." His jaw tensed and Sophia was afraid he was going to strike the wall again. "I'm going to go downstairs to talk to the ME. She took a night shift so she could examine Officer Murphy's body and wait for the blood results."

"Can I stay here?" Sophia asked, eyeing the room they had Amanda temporarily in. "I think Marina might need a little support."

Braydon's phone vibrated in his hand. He looked down at the number and back at her. She could tell that, if he could, the detective would shrink her and place her in his pocket for protection. However, seeing as she was a full grown woman, he couldn't very well do that. Though he looked as though he was about to try.

"Detective," someone called. "Detective?" They turned to see the doctor standing in the doorway of Amanda's room. "She's conscious." He didn't have to say anything else. Braydon and Sophia were already running toward him.

"She's awake?" Braydon asked, stopping as the doctor held up his hand to halt them.

"Just barely. You have less than one minute before we wheel her out." He turned to Sophia. "You need to stay out here."

"But—" Sophia started to complain.

"This woman has been put through hell. The only reason I'm even letting the detective in is because it could potentially save another life." Braydon went into the room without a look back. Sophia nodded and moved against the wall to try and listen. Thankfully there were no other patients in the rooms on either side making the task easier. More than anything she wanted to be in that room, but she stayed strong, remembering that it wasn't just Lisa's life on the line.

"Amanda?" Sophia heard Braydon ask. "Was it Nathanial Williams, a man with dark red hair, who took you?"

Sophia's body was still, her heart thumping in tandem with her anxiety.

"Yeah," Amanda croaked out, voice hoarse.

"Where was he keeping you?"

The woman was struggling to answer—that much Sophia could tell.

"Dunno."

"We believe that Nathanial also took Lisa Hardwick. Did you see her? Is she still alive?"

Sophia felt time slow. *This is it,* she thought. She braced herself against the wall, waiting for a stranger to give her hope or destroy it.

"Lisa's there," she said simply.

"But is she alive?" Braydon prodded.

Every fiber of Sophia's being stood up, waiting for the answer she had sought since Day One in Culpepper. Amanda Alcaster didn't realize it then, but what she was about to say was going to change Sophia's life. In one way or another, she was about to know of her sister's fate. "Amanda, is Lisa alive?"

"Yes," Amanda said so low that she almost missed it. "But, he wants Sophia."

Marina Alcaster must have broken the speed of light to get to the hospital. Seconds after Amanda's ominous message, she flew into the ER in a bout of tears and high-pitched squeals. Sophia wordlessly waved her over and had only a second to move out of the woman's way.

"My baby!" she yelled, hysterical. "I'm so sorry about our fight. I don't care about that land more than you! I love you, baby!"

The second nurse went in then and said Amanda was ready for surgery. Marina, knowing nothing of her daughter's condition, was told to follow them to the doctor but then she would have to go back to the lobby to wait. Not once did the older woman look at Sophia, though Braydon followed her to the end of the hallway quickly explaining the situation.

Lisa was still alive. It was a thought that made Sophia's heart soar. After all the time that had passed since she'd been taken, she was still alive. Not only was she alive, but they knew for a fact who had her.

"I feel like I can breathe a bit easier now," she admitted to Braydon when he made his way back. Lines of worry were etched across his forehead, each a cavern of concern.

"He wants you" was his response. His tone was cold. Sophia wanted to ease the detective's stress but knew there wasn't a thing she could do.

"I need to tell Richard," she said instead. "Go ahead and talk to the ME. I want to stay here to see how the surgery goes."

Braydon managed to tense up even more.

"I'm not leaving you alone," he said.

"And I don't want to see any more dead bodies," she snapped back before letting out a long sigh. "Sorry, I'd just rather stay up here for now." That didn't seem to change his resolve, so she added what she hoped was reassurance. "Listen, there's a full staff on this floor, in-

cluding security." She motioned to the hospital security
officer who had appeared after all the commotion. He
stood talking to a nurse at the nurses' station at the end
of the hall. "I'll be fine for a few minutes."

Braydon, ever the protective man, waged an internal
battle. His eyes never left hers.

"Fine," he relented. "But you stay here and call me if
anything and I mean *anything* happens. Okay?" She nodded. "Be safe." He waited a moment more before turning
and walking over to the elevator, already pulling out his
phone to make some calls. She watched him disappear
behind its doors.

Sophia went to reach for her own cell but realized,
too late, that it was still attached to its charger on the
detective's nightstand. She sighed and made her way to
the nurses' station.

"May I use the phone?" she asked the nurse behind the
partition. The woman obliged and even went so far as to
walk away and give her some privacy, the security guard
following her lead. Privacy. Something that would have
been rare in the city, Sophia thought fleetingly.

Richard answered on the first ring and after she broke
the news, he told her that nothing but the devil himself could stop him from coming to the hospital. Even if
Amanda was in surgery, he wanted to be there. Sophia
knew the feeling. Amanda was the closest they had been
to Lisa in days.

The traumatized woman was their first real link to
Nathanial, too. If she didn't make it, then finding the
madman and her sister would continue to be horribly difficult. Sophia fell into a lobby chair and put her head in
her hands. The image of her name etched into Amanda's
stomach was stuck in her mind like glue. What was Na-

thanial playing at? If he did get Sophia, what horrible things would he do to her?

"Oh, I can't take this," Sophia said aloud, standing. The news had been good to hear but now horrible images of what the madman could do raced through her head. Marina Alcaster was still nowhere to be found and so there was nothing to distract her.

"Could you tell Marina Alcaster, the woman who just ran in here, that I'll be right back to talk with her?" Sophia asked the nurse who had let her borrow the phone. She had decided that, dead body or not, she wanted to know as much about this case as she could. It was better than just sitting around and imagining the worst. Plus, she doubted Nathanial would show up at the hospital of all places. He'd have to know Braydon would be with her and that the detective would be more than willing to cause the man harm. "My name's Sophia. I'm friends with Detective Thatcher." The nurse agreed to give Marina the news and then told Sophia how to get to the room where Braydon and the ME would be talking. When the elevators took too long, Sophia headed to the stairs with a newfound purpose to her stride.

The medical examiner had an office in the basement of the building. It also happened to be smack-dab in the middle of the morgue. Sophia realized that made sense but it didn't put her nerves at ease. Each step she took downward was more nerve-racking than the last. She half expected a little girl from a horror movie to pop out just as the lights burned out. Once she was at the ground level, she almost sang with relief.

The hospital's basement was the polar opposite of the ground floor. It was like a wasteland. Sophia crept down the hallway, getting halfway through it and still not spotting a single soul. The lights that buzzed overhead were

more loud than bright and more annoying than helpful.
Instead of bouncing off all the white surfaces, they cast
shadows on everything.

"I wouldn't suggest you run," said a voice from behind
just as she passed another light emitting a high-pitched
buzz. "That action wouldn't bode well for your sister."

Sophia spun around. She should have listened to Braydon and stayed put on the first floor.

Nathanial Williams was standing in the mouth of the
hallway, smiling from ear to ear. He was nothing like the
man she had met before—the warm, inviting personality
had burned out and in its place was a man on the brink of
madness. Shadows crept around him as if he were creat-
ing them; they poured out over his facial features, forg-
ing a sinister mask with eyes as dark as coal. Maybe it
was just her imagination. Maybe Nathanial didn't look
different at all. Maybe now she knew too much about the
man to ever see him for anything other than a monster.

He stayed still as she looked him up and down. He
wore a blue janitor's jumpsuit with a faded name tag. In
his right hand was a black rectangular box.

Sophia didn't know which emotion would spring
out first, but she was glad it was anger before fear. She
straightened her back.

"Where is Lisa?" she asked The distance between
them made her feel much more confident than she should
when in the presence of a brilliant killer.

"Your sister? Oh, it doesn't matter. She won't be there
for too long."

Fear pulled at the pit of Sophia's stomach. "What does
that mean?"

"It means, Miss Hardwick, that I have a proposition
for you." He waved the box in the air before sliding it
across the floor. It stopped a few feet from her.

"Where's Lisa?" she asked again, not moving an inch. Nathanial seemed to think the question was funny. He laughed—the sound was hollow.

"Miss Hardwick, I believe we've moved on from that particular question, but I suppose I'll humor you. She's somewhere and I won't tell you where. Will that answer work for now? I'm trying to strike up a deal with you to save your sister." He was speaking as if they were playing a game, and maybe it was to him.

"What kind of deal?" She practically spat out the words. His smile grew wider.

"Open the box first."

Sophia hesitated. The morgue was down the hall and to the left. If she ran fast enough Braydon might be able to catch up to the madman. At the very least, she bet if she yelled he would hear her. It wasn't as if anyone else was down on the floor with them.

"If you're stalling in the hopes that Detective Thatcher will magically appear, saving you in the nick of time, I would advise against it." He sighed. "Every second you *do not open that box* is one more second that I'll tick off of Lisa's life. Now open it or I'll leave before your knight in shining armor can stop me."

Sophia felt her confidence receding. She took a step forward and picked the box up. To her surprise, it was light. Inside was the most confusing combination of items. The first was a piece of red satin clothing, which, after a moment, she realized made up a dress. The second item was a small needle and syringe. It looked odd sitting in a sea of satin.

"What is this?" she asked.

"That, my dear Sophia, is my offer. I want to make a trade."

"What kind of trade?"

He was almost giddy when he spoke next. "You for your sister, of course." Sophia was almost certain her eyebrow had disappeared into her hairline. The man wasn't making the most sense. He held up his finger to keep her questions at bay.

"Let me elaborate." He cleared his throat. Despite the distance between them, it sounded as though he was right in front of her. "You may or may not have figured out that my ultimate plan is to make your detective suffer."

"Revenge," she stated.

"I wouldn't call it that per se, but I'm not going to stand here and say that you're wrong."

"But why? Braydon didn't kill Terrance. There's no revenge to be had. You need to accept that," she tried.

"I've also been asked to accept that God is real, but that doesn't mean I have." His smile cracked. "I do have my own set of beliefs, although they may not be religious in nature, they still ring true—Braydon Thatcher damned my family, Miss Hardwick. There isn't a force in this world that could convince me otherwise. So, if I were you, I'd stop right there."

A coldness settled in the pit of her stomach. In that moment she realized her own truth—Nathanial Williams would never see reason. He had left all sanity behind. If he'd ever had any at all.

"Okay, so where were we? Oh, right, destroying Detective Thatcher!" His cheerful smile returned. "On Sunday, Richard Vega will be throwing the annual Culpepper Fund-raiser. I want you to tell him to make sure it stays on course and I want you to attend." He pointed to the box. "Wearing that lovely little number."

"What? Why?" she couldn't stop from asking. It was a bizarre request that didn't fit the situation.

"At the fund-raiser I will trade you for your sister." He

paused, waiting for Sophia to respond, but she couldn't find the words. He then continued, unperturbed. "That is *if* you wear that dress. You may have also already realized that I'm a fan of theatrics. See, over the years my world has been submerged in numbers and theories and formulas. It instilled a secret love of all things dramatic within me and I just can't help but employ my own version of poetic justice against the man who ruined my family. Sure—" he took a step closer and stopped "—I could have killed Thatcher without all of this fuss and, sure, I could just kill you right here, right now, but there's honestly no fun in it for me. I want the *drama*. I want the *suffering*." Nathanial seemed to be vibrating with excitement. Sophia's confidence had completely gone and fear housed itself inside her very core. She dared not speak. She dared not breathe. The man kept his monologue going—a broadcast that couldn't be muted.

"You, however, were not in the original plan. I took Lisa with every intention of keeping her just out of Braydon's reach while making him look a fool in front of Mr. Richard Vega, who I've heard, makes no issue about taking down those who displease him. I meant to cripple Braydon's career by torturing and then killing the lover of the town's most powerful man. Then, when he was completely crushed, I would finish what I came here to do, but then I saw the way he looked at you—the way he cared. I saw a way to cut him deeper. I want you, Sophia, not your sister. Everyone else, the women of unfortunate timing, mean nothing to me now. Only you do and that's why I'm presenting you with an option here. I'd like to tell you I'm not as cruel as you think—I want to give you the chance to save your flesh and blood because I know the pain of having them taken." Sophia wanted to point out that her death would leave Lisa in the same boat, but held her tongue. The man seemed to be finishing his long speech. "You show up to the fund-raiser and I'll let Lisa go."

That was the bottom line.

"Why take me at the fund-raiser?" she finally managed.

"Because when I take you, I want it to be a challenge… one that, when I successfully pull it off, will make Braydon feel even more desolate."

"How do I even know Lisa's still alive?" It was one thing to hear it from Amanda. She wanted assurance from the man himself.

"I'll let you see her one more time. Give you a moment to say goodbye. Again, Miss Hardwick, I'm not a monster." Sophia had every doubt in the world about that. "Now, let's talk about that syringe before your friendly neighborhood detective comes back." He took his finger and pressed it to a spot on the side of his neck. "I want you to grab that needle and put it right here on your neck."

Sophia didn't have to ask what was in it. She knew it was his sleep-inducing cocktail.

"It won't kill you, but if you don't inject yourself with it I *will* kill your sister. Of that you can be completely certain." The smile oozed off of his face as he said it. "Braydon will think you're dead when he finds you. He'll get a taste of his future."

Sophia's world slowed. Her vision blurred. She hadn't taken the drug yet but she knew he had already won. With shaking hands she took out the syringe and stared into the eyes of a man filled with hate.

"Right now, you're probably thinking of saying something to the effect of Braydon Thatcher will, undoubtedly, stop me. That he'll save Lisa and then you, but remember, Sophia—he didn't stop me from killing Trixie, he didn't stop me from cutting up Amanda, and he didn't stop Terrance from killing his sister. I suggest, once more, you heed my advice. It's the only way to save your sister."

Sophia didn't hesitate this time. She placed the needle against her neck and pushed the liquid into her body.

"You're heartless," she said as cold pain began to spread through her. Nathanial laughed once more as his joyful smile returned.

"You're wrong, Sophia," he said. "I have a heart and that's the problem."

Chapter Fourteen

Officer Murphy had been helpless to defend himself as Nathanial choked the life out of him. The medical examiner confirmed that the same drug that had disabled Trixie had been found in the cop's bloodstream. Braydon reasoned that he had opened the door to question the man and had been stabbed with the needle before he was able to do anything more.

"I haven't heard back yet about what specific drug it is, but I think it's a safe bet that it's the one Nathanial was working on while at Microne," she had said after being filled in on the man's academic and work background. "He must have taken quite a few samples with him when he left. The best I can do right now is to equate the drug to Ambien which is used to help insomniacs sleep. Though, this particular mix seems to work much, much faster."

Braydon didn't have to agree; the fact that two people hadn't had the time to fight back was proof enough of the drug's power. Instead he thanked the woman for her help and left. He didn't know what he had hoped for when he had come down. At least he could tell James's family that he hadn't been awake when he was killed. It wasn't a lot but the idea of a painless death might be comforting.

It was something he had wished Amelia had.

He brought his phone out and was about to call the captain to tell him the news when something down the hall caught his eye.

"Sophia!"

Instant fear exploded in his chest as he closed the distance between them, his heart already thumping at a nauseating pace. The way she was sprawled on the ground, unnaturally still, tore a wound inside him open, letting an overwhelming feeling of anguish pour out. He couldn't lose her. He wouldn't lose her.

He crouched down next to her, immediately checking to see if she was breathing. For one long second her chest didn't rise and the world seemed to darken because of it, but then she took in a breath and let one out. It was the most beautiful thing he had ever seen.

"Sophia?" he tried again, quickly scanning her body for any blood or obvious marks. His eyes stopped on her neck where a small red bump had formed.

His fear for her life switched gears as he realized that the man who had done this to her wasn't far off. He pulled out his gun and with his free hand dialed Tom.

As soon as his partner answered, Braydon started talking, "Nathanial is in the hospital, or was. He drugged Sophia. We're on the bottom floor."

"I'm pulling into the parking lot now" was Tom's response before Braydon disconnected. The urge to search for Nathanial seared through him but he would not leave Sophia alone.

With one more look around, he put his gun back in its holster and carefully pulled her into his arms, trying to ignore her absolute lack of resistance. It was then that he noticed the box at her feet. Without putting her down he managed to kick off the lid. Inside was an empty syringe atop red material. He didn't have the time to look in any more detail. There was no guarantee that what she had been injected with was the same drug as the others. Sophia needed help as soon as possible. Braydon refused to lose her.

With as much caution as he could afford while still trying to hurry, he got her into the elevator and together they rode to the first floor. During the seconds between he focused on her breathing. It continued to be a beautiful sight.

The first floor of the hospital was in a frenzy. Cops, hospital security guards, and staff were bustling around forming one loud commotion. John the Ticketer ran up to them as soon as the elevator doors slid open. He yelled for help but instead of waiting for hospital staff to come to them, Braydon marched Sophia into one of the small ER rooms before depositing her on a bed. A doctor he recognized but whose name he couldn't place ran up and started to check her vitals while Braydon filled him in.

"Tom took the stairs to the basement and we have two bodies going through the second floor. A nurse called the ME and told her to lock her doors, too," John said as the doctor and a nurse worked. "The captain is outside and Cara just walked in."

Braydon nodded but kept his attention on Sophia. Her face was slack, her lips downturned. He wanted to touch them, to kiss them, until the sleeping woman awoke. The doctor turned and, on seeing his gaze, seemed to soften.

"Her vitals are normal. She's just asleep right now," he said. "I'll move her to a room to keep a better eye on her but, for now, she's fine."

A weight lifted from Braydon's chest and for one moment he felt pure elation. However, it didn't last long. He took a few steps out into the hall and called the woman officer over.

"Is she okay?" Cara asked, looking over his shoulder.

"For now. I need you to watch her," he said. "You do not leave her side for any reason, do you understand?" She nodded. "Once she's in that room only the captain or the doctor go in there."

"What are you going to do?"

"Nathanial is too smart to stick around. I'm going to go look at the security tapes to see if that can't help us somehow." Braydon cast one more look in Sophia's direction. "Don't let her out of your sight."

Finding a security guard wasn't hard since all of the hospital staff had been alerted. Braydon followed him to the room that held all the security feeds for the entire hospital and ordered him to play the ones from the bottom floor. The guard didn't seem to be offended at the lack of kindness in him and started to pull up the right tapes. Under Braydon's direction he rewound the footage to where Sophia exited the stairwell and then pressed Play. The two of them watched as she walked down the hallway while Nathanial walked behind her before stopping.

All Braydon saw was white-hot rage. It was as if he was eighteen again, the difference being instead of wanting to kill Terrance Williams, he was focused on his older, more sadistic brother. He looked at the computer monitor and willed the man he saw on its screen a horrific, slow death.

"Turn it up," Braydon barked out to the security guard. Sophia's lips were moving but he couldn't hear anything.

"I can't. The audio hasn't worked on these recordings in years." It took everything he had not to slug the guard.

"Then why haven't you had it fixed?"

"Look, man, we don't have that kind of money right

now," the guard defended. "Just be thankful this camera is working. Two more on the same floor have been down for weeks."

Braydon didn't say any more. Instead he watched the scene unfold on the security tape with rage boiling in his veins. There she was, caught in the killer's sights. Nathanial slid her a box and must have said something interesting enough to entice her to open it. Braydon knew now what was inside.

Even though they couldn't hear the exchange, Braydon continued to watch with heightened concentration, focusing on Sophia's facial expressions. When Nathanial had first stopped her, he could make out the stubborn anger that made her posture go straight. Then, the more Nathanial had talked, the more she had sagged at the weight of his words. Her apparent fear translated through the computer screen and right into his heart. Then, Nathanial pointed to his neck. There was more talk and, all of a sudden, she was injecting herself.

"She did it to herself," said the guard, just as Sophia crumpled to the ground. Braydon was completely taken aback. When he found Sophia he had assumed she had been given the injection against her own will.

Braydon swore as Nathanial walked over to Sophia's prone body. He knelt next to her and brushed the hair off her face. Then he turned and looked straight into the camera. With a smile that almost mirrored his brother's, he waved.

"Why did he do that?" the guard asked.

Braydon was so angry it felt as if his body was vibrating. "He wanted me to see him." Nathanial left Sophia and went to the elevator where he rode to the main lobby and walked right out through the front doors of the hospital.

John the Ticketer came into the room then and was ordered to stay with the guard and find out when Nathanial had come in.

"I also want to know how he came in, if he talked to anyone, and if he made any detours," he ordered. "You don't leave this room until you figure all of that out, okay?"

John nodded and then Braydon turned to the security guard. "I want you to make sure that man does not come back into this hospital. You notify every staff member on shift. I don't care if you have to go to every damn room to do it, either. If you see him, you call me *immediately*. Got it?"

"Yessir."

"Good." He gave the man his cell number and went back to Sophia's new room. Officer Whitfield was standing guard at the door, currently being yelled at by Richard Vega.

"You know I'm not the killer, for heaven's sakes!" he yelled, throwing his hands into the air in frustration.

"I'm sorry, Mr. Vega. I'm not supposed to let anyone in here unless authorized by Detective Thatcher or Captain Westin."

"I'm only here because Sophia called me—" He stopped midrant when he saw Braydon arrive.

"You can't talk to her now," Braydon said, glazing over any greeting. He didn't have time. Sophia was a few feet away, unconscious in a hospital bed. Just because the doctor said she would be fine didn't mean she wasn't still in danger.

"I'm guessing he's no longer here," Richard said after a moment.

Braydon didn't respond. He didn't have to. The two men glanced at the room next to them.

"What do we do now, then?" Richard wanted to know.

"We find the bastard."

THERE WAS A TICKING AGAIN—a clock saying to the world it knew exactly what time it was and it wanted everyone to know. Sophia hated it. She wished it would shut up. Clocks in Culpepper were the bane of her existence as far as she was concerned. She opened her eyes to find the source of her annoyance and was surprised at how hard it was to do—each lid was heavy and, once up, wanted very badly to go back down.

"Sophia?" a man asked at her side. Even in the haze she was currently seeded in, she knew it wasn't Braydon. This man was shorter and had blond hair. Her eyes slowly slid to Richard's mouth. It held a small smile. "How do you feel?"

She looked around the hospital room and thought about that for a second. Like opening her eyes, this was also a difficult task.

"Awake" was all she could come up with as an answer. Richard laughed.

"Well, I suppose that's good."

She nodded and her head swam at the movement. She shut her eyes tight until the world settled. The clock continued to tick.

"Do you remember what happened?" Sophia opened her eyes at his abrupt change in tone. It softened to almost a whisper. His face was as open as she had ever seen it— kind and patient. He was dressed down in a plain T-shirt and jeans, looking nothing like he had the first time she'd met him. He looked like just a regular guy. "Sophia?"

She realized she was staring.

"Sorry, everything's kind of fuzzy," she admitted. He came to the side of her bed and patted her hand.

"I'd imagine so—you've been out for almost thirteen hours." She didn't have the speed to react with a worthy response. He seemed to realize this and patted her hand once more. "It's okay. Don't rush it. I'll go get the doctor."

Sophia watched him go. She wondered where Braydon was but wasn't quick enough to answer. It was as though she was submerged underwater. Everything felt slow. What *did* happen? The last thing she clearly remembered was kissing Braydon in the kitchen—the thought made her cheeks heat despite whatever weird fog she was in— but she knew that wasn't the last thing that happened. She scrunched up her face in concentration.

That's when she remembered a grin that made her blood run cold.

Nathanial.

SOPHIA COULD HEAR Braydon running down the hall toward her room. Cara paused what she was doing.

"Want me to tell him to hold on until we're done?" she asked.

"Please." Sophia leaned back against the bed and waited while Cara slipped outside to hold off the detective. She could hear his annoyed tone as he agreed to stay put. Cara came back in, careful to shut the door quickly, and went back to Sophia's side to finish the task they'd started.

"Thanks again for helping me with this. I don't think the nurse likes me much." Sophia held on to Cara as the officer steered them to the bathroom.

"No problem. When you gotta go, you gotta go."

It had been almost a half hour since Sophia had woken from her drug-induced sleep. The doctor had come in twice to check her vitals and, with a lot of head scratching, he had declared her as healthy as a horse. The only way the doctor would allow her to leave was for her to give them a urine sample they could test. Sophia didn't have any room to argue and two bottles of water later, she was about to burst.

The only problem was that her limbs didn't seem to want to function together. Her legs quaked like jelly when she attempted to stand on her own. Whatever had made her mind fuzzy had made her body just as sluggish. It had been a blessing that Braydon had assigned Cara to watch the room. She suspected he had noticed the friendship that had formed between them. The bathroom trip just made it more official.

When the mission was complete and the sample collected, Sophia sat in one of the two armchairs next to the bed. She didn't want to look so helpless when Braydon came in.

"Are you good now?" Cara asked. "Ready for Detective Thatcher?" There was a smile in her voice, though her face remained serious. Sophia had told Richard and Cara the same story about her run-in with Nathanial. She wanted them to understand how unbalanced, and therefore dangerous, the man was.

"Yes, thank you. Send in the bull," Sophia teased. She wanted the mood to lighten if only for a second. Cara finally smiled, then slipped out as Braydon came in.

"Hi," Sophia greeted. She meant it to sound strong but couldn't deny its smallness. Braydon stopped next to her and openly looked up and down her body. She adjusted her hospital gown subconsciously. The detective, apparently approving of what he saw, grabbed the other chair and moved it so he was sitting right in front of her. They were so close their knees were touching.

"Tell me what happened," he said. The time for playing was over. Braydon Thatcher was a man on a mission, except his had nothing to do with bathroom functions. His was much more dangerous.

"Cara said you watched the security footage," she started.

"But there was no sound."

"So...you want to know why I injected myself."

He nodded, his jaw set hard. "Yes, I want to know why you injected yourself instead of running, yelling for help or even attacking him."

"You're mad at me."

"You're damn right I am!" he yelled, standing. "You could have died, Sophia! What could that man have said that would make you think what you were doing was a good idea?" There was no mere undercurrent of disapproval in his voice—it was a tidal wave rushing across the surface. He wasn't going to like what she had to say. She sighed before recounting what had happened. She didn't stop once, ignoring the fists he had balled on his knees.

"What if he'd been lying about what was in there? You could have died, Sophia," he said, bringing his voice down and sitting back in his chair. "Then where would we be?" Sophia flinched at his words but her resolve stood firm. She didn't know who the "we" was but she knew it wasn't the time to ask.

"Remember when you told me you *knew* Nathanial was dangerous?" She waited for him to calm down enough to nod. "Well, I *knew* he wasn't going to kill me. I did what he told me because I also *knew* that if I didn't he would have killed Lisa."

"Sophia—"

She put her hand against his cheek. "Please don't be mad at me for what I did," she said, voice low. "It was a gamble that I wasn't ready to lose. You tell me you wouldn't have done the same thing."

"I would have killed him," he responded, though his tone was calm again.

"Well, all I had was a syringe. If I had messed it up, he probably would have killed me right then before going to do the same to Lisa." She dropped her hand back into her lap—holding it up had been a feat all its own while Nathanial's drug worked its way out of her system. "Plus, he's right—only he knows where Lisa is. If he had died and we couldn't find her, I would have blamed myself for the rest of my life."

Braydon sat still as another internal battle waged within him. Sophia waited for the victor to show. She knew he understood why she had listened to Nathanial but the protective part of him was screaming that the risk had been too high. The conflicting viewpoints waged behind his pools of blue. Eventually, the more reasonable side won.

"Just don't do it again, okay? That's all I ask." Sophia nodded but now she had to approach a more delicate topic.

"What Nathanial wants me to do…you know I have to do it." Braydon's eyes almost bugged out of their sockets while his lips stretched thin.

"You aren't seriously wanting to go to the fund-raiser are you?"

"I wouldn't use the word *want* but yes, I *am* going." Her voice was calm—level in sincerity.

"Sophia, he's asked you to hand yourself over."

"I don't have a choice," she pointed out.

"Yes, you do," he stressed. "Sophia, he isn't asking you to go watch a movie or to take a stroll around the god-damn park. He wants you so he can torture you *before* he kills you. He wants to kill you as my punishment. *My* punishment." He grabbed both of her hands. "There's no question about if he'll keep you alive or not. He won't. He'll only let you live long enough to torture you. That's all." There was fire in his eyes. Sophia hoped she had the same fierce gaze placed on him.

"Then don't let him take me," she said. "Let's take Lisa instead."

BRAYDON KNEW THAT the younger Hardwick woman wasn't going to budge on her decision to attend the Culpepper Fund-raiser. If he was honest about it, he already knew what her choice would be before she said it out loud. She loved her sister with a passion that the threat of death couldn't destroy and would stop short of nothing to prove it. He respected her immensely for it, though he tried a few more times to talk her out of Nathanial's trap. She, of course, refused to reconsider. So instead of beating that dead horse, Braydon switched into planning mode.

He excused himself, or rather was shooed out of the room so Cara could help Sophia change, and found Richard down the hallway. He was staring at a vending machine with his hands in his pockets and mind somewhere else entirely. It took him a few seconds to realize Braydon was standing next to him.

"Sophia told you everything?" he asked, eyes still on the rows of candy bars.

"Yes."

"I'm assuming you're not comfortable with her plan?" he asked, looking at the detective.

"It's not *her* plan, it's his." Braydon was trying not to sound accusatory but he couldn't stop what he said next. "Are you comfortable with her plan? Her life for Lisa's?" He knew it wasn't a fair question to ask but he didn't know where the man stood. Richard had Lisa while Sophia was single. To the general public she didn't have someone who had her back. "Because I can't help but hate the plan." He didn't like the idea that he was the only person stepping forward in an attempt to fight the deadly idea of her sacrifice. He wanted her and everyone else to know that he *was* in fact defending her. Richard took a moment before he answered. For once, it didn't sound full of his normal energy.

"Do you know I'd never met Sophia before the other day?" He didn't wait for Braydon to answer. "I hadn't even talked to her on the phone until after Lisa went missing. She didn't like when we started seeing each other and she certainly didn't approve that we kept on dating. That alone could give me reason to not like her, but…" His face became thoughtful as he searched for his next words. "I feel like I've always known her. They may have been at odds lately, but that never stopped Lisa from telling me all about her little sister. After a while I realized she didn't even notice that she was telling me stories about Sophia. She would see or hear something that reminded her of this memory or that memory and then tell me all about it. For instance, every time we get into bed at night she throws all of the pillows on the floor and smiles. Do you know why?" Braydon shook his head. "When they were young, Lisa used to fill up their bedroom floor with all of her pillows and Sophia hated it, for a while at least. Then Lisa would pull her down on top of them and they'd laugh, Sophia would smile and everything would be fine again. However, one night Lisa told me a secret—she hated the piles of pillows. When *she* was little, Lisa had a bad habit of rolling off the bed in the middle of the night. She became so afraid that she would roll off and hurt herself that she stopped sleeping altogether. So, her dad bought her enough pillows to cover the floor while she slept to cushion the ground, just in case. She didn't think it would work so he demonstrated, rolling off onto them. It became a nighttime ritual, she said, but then he died. She said she hated the sight of the pillows after that."

"Why did she keep them, then?" Braydon asked, genuinely curious.

"Because one day a very young Sophia cried about not remembering her father. She was a toddler when he died so she didn't have the memories that Lisa did. Their mother had no business being a mother and didn't know or care about helping the little girl. So, when Sophia wouldn't stop crying, Lisa did what her father had done every night before bed and rolled onto the ground over and over again until Sophia finally stopped." Richard smiled. "It may not seem like that much of a story but after all of these years Lisa could have told Sophia that the whole routine used to make her sad—make her miss her father—but instead she's kept the act up and even stocks her house *and* mine with tons of odd pillows because in her words 'Sophia deserves them.' Lisa believes with all of her heart that Sophia deserves to always be happy. So, you tell me, Detective, do you think Lisa would say that Sophia deserves to be brutally killed by a sadistic man?"

"No," he answered.

"Then why would I?"

Chapter Fifteen

Sophia felt 50 percent better once the hospital gown was off. There was something about the way they looked that set her on edge. Maybe it was the fact that if a person was wearing one it meant they were in the hospital and therefore not in the best of shape. Either way, after Cara helped her into her normal clothes, she gave a loud sigh of relief.

"You okay?" Cara asked.

"All things considered, yes." She sat down in one of the chairs and went to work putting on one of her shoes. The doctor guessed the drug would leave her tired and wobbly for a few more hours but she would fully recover. He equated Nathanial's injection to taking one very large sleeping pill before chasing it down with some whiskey. Sophia could attest to this assessment—her body wasn't as off-kilter as it had been, but she wouldn't be passing any field sobriety tests in the near future. Good thing she was already in the hands of the Culpepper PD. "I still can't believe I was out for almost *thirteen* hours. I guess Nathanial knew what he was doing when he made this stuff." She quieted as guilt pushed out her next question. "How's Amanda doing? Braydon said she still hasn't woken up."

"The doctor said she had a lot more of that stuff in her system but they were able to stop the bleeding and stitched her up good. So that's a plus," Cara said. She tossed Sophia's wayward right shoe at her. "Since she was injected before y'all brought her in, they think she'll wake up by tonight. Marina sure hasn't left her side, though. I've never known that woman to be quiet this long. It kind of makes me nervous."

"It's good that she's staying with her."

"Yeah, normally you can hear the two of them fussing at each other from a mile away but...I think they're pretty close when you get down to it."

"That's a relationship I can understand." Sophia smiled.

"We're also leaving them an officer just in case." She folded her arms across her chest as her face hardened. The last officer they had left to guard someone had ended up dead, but they both knew it wouldn't play out like that with Amanda. Nathanial had made it clear that he only had eyes for Sophia.

"I'm glad she's going to make it," she said truthfully. "I just hope her stomach doesn't scar." Cara gave her a sympathetic look. They both knew it would. She felt guilty that Amanda had been used as a personal message to her and Braydon. It also didn't help that it was her name that had been cut into the woman's skin.

The doctor came soon after and gave Sophia the okay to leave, though he tried to make her stay for observation at least twice. Braydon took over helping her walk to the truck. His closeness allowed his beautiful scent to envelop her. It stirred up the feelings from their first kiss, which felt like a lifetime ago. The thought sent a pleasant tingle through her. She was almost sad when he helped her into the cab. Cara, though off duty, followed behind the truck as they left the hospital.

"Where are we going?" she asked, settling into her

seat. Once again, she marveled at how familiar this routine had become.

"Back to my place for the moment. I didn't have a chance to grab your things earlier today."

What with a crazed man dropping a half-dead woman on the porch, she thought.

"Then where are you putting me?" She was half teasing. It seemed like every time she had gotten into his truck he had taken her somewhere new.

"You and Cara will be headed to Château Vega."

"Isn't Cara off duty?" she asked. It wasn't fair to keep sticking the officer with her if she didn't have to.

"Everyone on the force is working this case, off duty or not." There was a note of pride for his peers in his tone. "Small towns are stereotypically close, remember? If you mess with one of us, you mess with all of us."

"How much *does* the town know of what's been going on?" She hadn't had the chance to really wonder how everything that happened looked on the outside. She suspected that, under different circumstances, she wouldn't have been kept in the loop of knowledge during the investigation. Plus, aside from the hospital, she hadn't really been anywhere truly public without an officer or Braydon. If there was gossip going around Culpepper it fell on deaf ears where Sophia was concerned.

"After James's death, Captain Westin made an announcement about Nathanial being a dangerous man and to take safety precautions until we have him in custody. Knowing how unstable he really is now, I'm glad we let the town know that he's running around."

"And what about Lisa and Amanda?"

"We've tried to keep their names out of the public, if only because people around here can get really riled up and turn into vigilantes." He sighed. "Normally, it might be a good thing to have an entire town looking for them, but it's too much of a risk with Nathanial. He has no empathy—if someone got in his way, he'd only drag them into his little play of evil." She had to agree there. Culpepper had already lost enough because of the man. "Richard and Marina kept quiet as best they could but, you know how gossip is—I'm sure it isn't as much of a secret as we want it to be."

She nodded and yawned. The Nathanial Cocktail was one heck of a drug.

"So why are Cara and I going to Richard's?"

"I'm not comfortable with the security at Lisa's or my place anymore," he said bitterly. "Richard already has guards and a gate."

"He has guards?" she asked incredulously. Was Richard *that* big of a man that he needed not one but multiple people to watch over him?

"He has two on rotation year-round—cousins Able and Dwight Stevens. He brought them with him when he moved here. They live in a house at the back of the property with Able's wife. From what I know of them, they're pretty dependable guys. Honestly, I should have taken you there instead of my place." He paused, about to say something, but then stopped himself. He turned his neck to the side and popped it before continuing. "I guess I just felt better with you near me."

Sophia felt herself blush, but wasn't embarrassed by it. She was used to the effect he had on her and didn't care to make excuses for it. Instead, she turned to face him and smiled.

"I felt better, too." That seemed to ease his mind. He didn't smile but he stopped frowning. "So, while we're at Richard's where will you be?"

"Hunting."

The house at 2416 Gothic Street hadn't changed in the past seventeen hours or so since they had been gone but to Sophia it felt like a different world. Captain Westin was sitting on the front porch looking down at the spot where Amanda had been when they pulled into the driveway. Sophia felt more confident in her abilities to walk alone. She shooed off the helping hands of Braydon and Cara and walked right up to the captain and shook his hand. He returned the gesture with a firm grip.

"Glad to see you're okay, Hardwick," he boomed. "Pretty gutsy move you pulled."

"Thanks," she said, "at least I think."

"Don't worry, that was a compliment," Braydon whispered just over her shoulder. His breath tickled the exposed skin of her neck. Suddenly she was self-conscious of the fact that she'd been holed up in a hospital bed all day without a shower or a good teeth-brushing.

"Right," she said, making sure to turn her breath away from the man. She excused herself to his room and began to pack up her things. When the EMTs were loading Amanda into the ambulance, she and Braydon had grabbed a change of clothes to throw on in lieu of their pajamas or, in Braydon's case, the lack thereof. He had flung open his chest of drawers, grabbed a pair of jeans and a black shirt then put them on as he ran back outside. Sophia had taken more time with her jeans and tank top. Now, standing in the middle of the room, she looked at the combined mess they had made in their hurry. It was like a small bomb had gone off.

"You okay?" Braydon popped around the corner. She could hear Captain Westin and Cara talking in the living room.

"Yeah. I'm just…sorry for making such a mess." She didn't know why, but at the moment she was pushing down the urge to start cleaning the entire room. Because *that* made sense. Braydon began to laugh.

"You didn't make a mess. I believe it was me who did all of that." He pointed to the pile of clothes on the floor. "Plus, my bedroom floor is usually covered with clothes anyway." Sophia felt her eyes narrow in abrupt jealousy, imagining women's clothes littering the room. Which was a reaction, she reasoned again, that didn't make sense to have in their situation. The detective cleared his throat and quickly continued, "I mean I *am* a single guy living by himself. It's normal for me." He rubbed the back of his neck and tried to act as if he hadn't purposely thrown the word *single* in for her benefit. Sophia's eyes reverted to round and amicable. It was nice to know that Detective Braydon Thatcher wasn't swimming around the dating pool. Especially since they had shared a kiss—one that Sophia couldn't quite get out of her head.

She finished packing and together they went outside to Cara's 4Runner. Braydon put her bag in the backseat and stood with the passenger door open as she scooted into the seat. Cara sent a questioning look to Sophia, then to the detective when she, too, got into the car.

"I want you two to be careful—to be safe, okay?" He looked between the women, then to Cara. "Don't play hero if you see him." Then, very noticeably he inclined his head to Sophia. "Got it?"

"Yessir."

He gave her a quick smile. "You know the drill then, call me—"

"If I need anything or anything happens," she finished.

"Exactly. Let me know when you two get to Richard's. I'll stop by later." He shut the door after one prolonged shared look with Sophia and headed back inside. An odd feeling of loneliness moved against her chest but she shook it off. There were more important things happening than her selfish feelings for the man with aquamarine eyes.

Chapter Sixteen

Braydon ran a hand through his hair. He was standing in front of a closed door and wondering why he was even there. The afternoon had flown by with no new leads and them no closer to finding Nathanial or Lisa. Wherever he had her, it was one hell of a hiding place. The only person who could help them was still asleep in the hospital, though the doctors were positive she would wake up soon.

He sighed.

Amanda shouldn't be the only person who could help them break the case. He was a detective and, although newly appointed, he liked to think he was good at his job. However, the longer Lisa was out there—scared, possibly hurt and in the hands of a madman—he felt he was losing any claim he once had. Not only was he unable to stop Nathanial but he was now afraid he had lost Sophia's confidence.

She'd said she had injected herself because she'd known that Nathanial would kill Lisa if she didn't. In her mind, that only damned the sanity of "Terrance" Williams when in fact, it also quite clearly sent the message that she *knew* that Braydon wouldn't be able to find Lisa. It was a thought that frustrated him to no end.

He stood in the hallway of Richard Vega's second story. Cara and Richard were having a late-night dinner—both unable to sleep—while the Able cousins stood guard at each entrance to the house. The only other entrance was locked and between the two. If anyone managed to break in from that door they wouldn't be able to move throughout the house without one of the two seeing them first. Tom was sent home to rest for a while, the captain heading the search. Officers from the next county had been told to stay and help. Braydon hated the feeling of being useless. Maybe that was why he stood outside the bedroom Sophia was staying in. He wanted to comfort her, but at the same time he wanted to be comforted.

The realization made his mood sink lower. He didn't wait for guilt to rise in him—it had already surfaced and made a home after finding the body of Trixie Martin. Anger was its constant companion while an unhealthy sadness weighed down the edges of his mind. Having Nathanial's vendetta unveiled had made the memory of Amelia's death that much more prominent. Braydon hated to admit it, especially everything considered, but it made him miss her so much it hurt.

He let out a breath. It was almost midnight and Sophia was probably asleep. She didn't want or need him there. He had nothing new to deliver. With his mind made up, he turned to leave when he heard something that made him instantly reconsider—Sophia was awake and she was crying.

"Sophia?" He knocked on the door. "Are you okay?" There was some movement in the room but she answered right away.

"Yeah, hold on." His hand was already on the handle, but he waited until she gave the okay. "You can come in."

The guest bedroom was one of six in the entire house. It held a queen-size bed, a dresser and a love seat comfortably—all were pale pink and dark wood. Sophia was sitting on the love seat when he walked in, but the covers of the bed were pushed to the side and the floor was covered in pillows. She was trying to act normal but her swollen eyes and tear-streaked cheeks gave her away.

"What's wrong?" Braydon asked, immediately on alert. He had never seen the woman cry before—the aftermath was so unsettling he didn't realize at first she was only wearing a long T-shirt. Sophia tried on a smile, pushing her hair over her shoulder, but it slid right back off.

"I—" She paused and to Braydon's horror tears began to roll down her face. "I don't want to die," she finished, burying her face in her hands as she began to openly cry.

Braydon closed the space between them and knelt in front of her. He gently took her hands and pulled them away.

"You aren't going to die," he whispered. "I won't let you." He kissed her hands, keeping them in his own. She watched the movement while tears continued to come.

"But what if something happens tomorrow and—and he *does* get me," she said, close to sobbing. "He'll do awful things to me."

"Don't go, then. We can dress someone as you or—" He stopped as a loud sob escaped her.

"But then what if he kills Lisa?" she asked. "She's all I have!" She seemed to fold into herself at that, bringing her bare knees up to her chest. Braydon released her hands and took the seat next to her. Not caring if it was too brash of a movement, he put an arm around her shoulders and pulled her to him. She didn't protest and was soon leaning against his chest, his arms encircling her.

Up until that moment, Sophia Hardwick had been a rock. She had remained so calm, so collected, so confident. Sure, she had cried after finding Trixie but that had been an in-the-moment response—one that most any-one would have had. Since then she'd taken everything in stride, showing courage in the face of a madman who wanted nothing more than to see her dead. Braydon had liked her determination, her courage but, as she wept into his shirt, he realized that her vulnerability didn't dimin-ish her strength in the least. She was a strong woman who had finally let her worries catch up to her.

"Sophia," he said, stroking her hair, "he won't kill Lisa, and I know I can't keep asking you to trust me—I know I don't deserve it—but please believe me when I say that I will kill Nathanial before he ever gets a chance to hurt you." There was a hardness in his tone—a stone-cold promise he refused to ever break.

Sophia's sobs quieted and soon her tears ceased. She pulled back to look him in the eyes, but Braydon didn't drop his arms from around her.

"But I do trust you," she said, her voice and its mean-ing wonderful music to his ears. He smiled, relief flood-ing through him. "You're a good man, Braydon Thatcher. I hope you know that." He was about to respond but stopped when she leaned forward. Her lips pressed against his in a soft kiss.

At first he didn't return it—she was vulnerable—but then so was he. Bringing his hands to cup her face, he deepened the kiss, parting her lips with his tongue. She moaned into his mouth, which seemed to awaken the rest of his body. He wanted her—all of her.

"Wait," Sophia said, pulling away. Braydon froze. "Just, hold on." She stood up from the couch and walked to the door. He looked on, afraid they had gone too far, moved too fast. Then, she did something that made him give a little laugh.

She shut the door with a smile.

THERE WAS A KNOCK on the door. It was an annoying, continuous sound that brought Sophia out of her sleep and back into the real world. She stretched, thankful it wasn't a clock's ticking, and looked at the empty spot next to her. Instead of her spirits dropping at Braydon's absence, a smile bubbled up at the memory of his presence hours before.

She could still feel his lips on hers—their warmth, their passion. The way he had commanded her body's attention. It had been a long while since she'd been with a man, but, somehow, with Braydon it had been more than a physical connection.

Hunger had fused them together in a dance filled with much more than the need to momentarily escape their current situation. The way he had touched her, kissed her, held her…the way he had looked into her eyes. Sophia had felt a connection in those moments that she had never felt before—all encompassing and filled with fire.

The knock came again, pushing the memory of a perfect, naked-bodied Braydon to the back burner. Sophia let a sigh stream from her lips.

"Hold on," she called, stretching one last time. A pleasant soreness radiated throughout her body as she hurried around the room, grabbing clothes from her bag and putting them on. A quick glance at her phone showed that it was almost noon. That surprised her. She didn't think she would be able to sleep after doing nothing, thanks to Nathanial's drug. When she was finished dressing, she looked once more at the empty spot on the bed, then opened the door.

Cara stood in the hallway looking simply devious. She held up her hands. One held a cup of coffee and the other a chocolate muffin.

"I was sent here to try and coax you awake," she said.

"Who sent you?"

"Okay, fine, I sent myself," she confessed. "Braydon had me at the end of the hall to give you some space, but Jordan came around and has been talking to me for almost two hours and I just can't take it anymore." Sophia stepped aside to let the woman into the room.

"Jordan?"

"Richard's nonstop-talking assistant. He keeps whining about every little thing while the vendors and decorators set up for tonight. Also, I think he's scared, too, and likes being around someone with a gun. I told him we had this place locked down but I guess some people are just naturally nervous. Though, I can't say I blame him right now. I hope it's okay that I woke you. I wasn't sure how much sleep you got." Sophia's eyes widened and heat started to spread up her neck as Cara glanced at the bed. She took in the rumpled sheets and pillows and, with more horror on Sophia's part, together they spotted a pair of wayward panties on the floor next to the foot of the bed. Cara was kind enough to pretend she didn't see any of it and instead sat on the love seat and held out the gifts she'd brought. Sophia gladly took them and joined her on the couch, the heat from her embarrassment ebbing away as the smell of coffee invaded her senses.

"Coffee is always appreciated where I'm concerned." She took a sip and almost sang, it was so good. Cara let her enjoy it for a moment before bringing reality into the room with them.

"Amanda Alcaster woke up early this morning," she began, instantly grabbing Sophia's attention. "Braydon already questioned her—he was adamant about being the first person to talk to her." Sophia nodded, glad that Braydon had been the one to do it. She trusted him, a fact that didn't surprise her anymore.

"What did she say? Does she know where Lisa is?"

"No, I'm afraid not, *but* she was able to give Braydon and Tom a new lead to track down…" She let her words trail off. There was something she didn't want to say.

"That's good, right?" If the lead came from Amanda, then surely it had to be good, she thought.

"Well, we now know why it's been so hard to find Nathanial. According to Amanda, someone is helping him."

Sophia almost spit her coffee out.

"What do you mean 'helping him'?"

"Amanda said they were kept in a windowless room, most likely in someone's house, and when Nathanial was down there with them, they could still hear someone moving around in the rest of the house. Sometimes they also heard him talking to someone but they never heard the other voice clearly enough." Sophia didn't know which piece of information to tackle first. Nathanial was partnered up with someone, but who would agree to be part of such a sinister plan? They were kept in a windowless room. What were the conditions there? Were they tied up? Were they abused? Cara seemed to pick up on the more intimate questions and continued. "Amanda said they were tied to chairs and were given bathroom breaks and food. She said Nathanial never hurt them."

"Except when he decided to carve my name into her stomach," Sophia said with anger.

"He had already put her to sleep when he did that." Cara sighed. "Small blessings I suppose." Sophia marveled that cutting someone up *after* they were asleep was a blessing at all, but in this case, it was true.

"So what lead did she give if she didn't know where they were being held?"

"We found out that Amanda had been talking to Nathanial when she was working at the gas station through

Tipsy's security tapes." Cara's whole demeanor changed as she started talking again—she was excited. "When we asked her about it she said that Nathanial had been talking to Amanda about buying the Dolphin Lot. He expressed interest one day and she ate it up. When her mama found out they had a big fight. She left, got a little drunk and went back home. Decided to let off some steam and walked back through the lot. She said Nathanial pulled up around then and grabbed her."

"That's what Marina was talking about in the hospital," Sophia started. "She said she loved Amanda more than that land!"

Cara nodded.

"He went through a lot of unnecessary trouble," she thought aloud. Sophia had to agree.

"Let's hope it's his love of theatrics that does him in."

Chapter Seventeen

There were two plans underway with the same goal—
take down Nathanial while saving both Hardwick sisters. However, the route to the finish line varied between
two methods.

The first plan hadn't changed since day one. Just because Nathanial had said the only way to save Lisa was
to make the trade, that didn't stop half the police force
from continuing to look for her. Unlike the first few days
of the women's disappearances, there was more confidence among the searchers. They knew about the connection between Nathanial and Amanda, knew the women
had been in a house, and knew that Nathanial was not
working alone. The last fact dimmed some enthusiasm
but at least now they could broaden their list of suspects
now that they were looking for more than just Nathanial.

Unfortunately, no one knew where Nathanial's car
was. Amanda had only been able to say that Lisa had said
it was old. Between the two of them, Nathanial hadn't
drugged Lisa immediately when he grabbed her. Captain Westin had some of his men finding regular Tipsy
patrons who had been seen on the security tapes that he
and Tom had gone through in hopes that they'd remember something about Nathanial's visits with Amanda.

The second plan, dubbed everyone's least favorite,

was built around Nathanial's trade. No matter how much they disliked the plan, they couldn't ignore it. Since Nathanial hadn't ordered Sophia to come to the fund-raiser alone, the plan was changed to Braydon's liking—instead of handing Sophia over so she could be taken away, tortured and killed, there would be a big ambush and the sisters would be saved. Until Nathanial contacted her, Sophia would attend the fund-raiser with Braydon and Cara at her side. The rest of the police force that weren't out actively searching would dress up in their formal best and mingle as if it was going out of style. Everyone would be on alert.

Everyone would have eyes on Sophia.

She hoped and prayed that the first plan would work, but as the sun went down and night fell over the once-sleepy town of Culpepper, it was time to prepare for option two.

Sophia stood in front of the mirror and looked at her reflection with a mix of anxiety and appreciation. She hated to admit it, but Nathanial's dress was beautiful.

It was a sheath dress, fitting against her body like a glove, and falling to the tops of her knees. Thin, silk straps held it up while the bust of the dress left little to the imagination—cutting low on her chest while simultaneously pushing her breasts high enough that her cleavage could be seen from a mile away. Under different circumstances, she would have loved to attend a swanky function wearing such a garment but she couldn't seem to get behind loving it while a crazy man waited for her. Though, again, she hated to admit that it looked and felt good against her skin. The ruby-red satin emphasized each curve of her body while the color mixed well with her complexion. On reflex alone, she applied some eyeliner and lipstick. Her hair she twirled up into a high bun. It made her feel more prepared for potential action.

"You ready in there?" Braydon called from the other side of the door. His voice sent a thrill through her.

"You can come in," she called back, taking one last look at her reflection. She wondered if it would be the last time she ever saw herself, a morbid thought that she tried to tamp down quickly.

"Wow." Braydon stood in the doorway, with an apparent look of appreciation. She gave him a polite smile.

"You don't look so bad yourself," she responded, walking over to him. He wore a black blazer that was opened up, showing a dark blue button-down. His slacks were also black and matched dark dress shoes. He was freshly shaved while the wild mane of hair she had grown used to in the past four days was slicked back with gel. His entire image had an effect just south of her waist, only made stronger by the memory of what was beneath each stretch of fabric that he wore.

"I knew I'd need to step up my game if I was going to deserve the company of my date." He grinned down at her. No matter how high her heels seemed to be, she was still under Braydon's gaze.

"Your date? Do I know her?" Sophia teased. It was Braydon's turn to roll his eyes.

"I'm sure you'll meet her. She's about your height, has these beautiful green eyes and is undeniably stubborn." He bent his head so that he whispered in her ear. "She also does this little trick in bed where—" Sophia laughed and slapped his chest.

"Okay, okay. I get it!" She took a step back while her cheeks cooled down. "Are there a lot of people here yet? I haven't really left the room all day." She had spent it worrying about Lisa. The night with Braydon seemed to have relieved the fear for her own life. She had cried, and done other things, until that fear had turned to determination—an even calm that left no room for second-guessing. Whatever happened tonight, she knew two things for certain: she would do anything for her sister and she would never blame anyone other than Nathanial if anything happened to Lisa.

"A few," he answered, "but none more beautiful than you."

The detective closed the space between them and wrapped his arms around her. They stood there for a time. The sound of the South played outside the window—frogs and insects stringing their respective sounds together for a chorus that only outsiders seemed to notice. Sophia took a deep breath in and let it out. Braydon kissed the top of her head, sending a wave of pleasure through her. It was the last calm before the storm.

They left the room and made their way downstairs. Sophia, Braydon and Cara walked out the front door and followed the path that led to the area of yard that had been sectioned off for the event. Valets were already standing at attention, ready to park the cars farther down the street, while caterers and Jordan, the newly appointed party planner since Lisa wasn't there, buzzed around, making sure everything was going according to plan.

Richard Vega knew how to throw a party; there were no two ways about it.

Sophia's nerves were on edge. She may have been resolute to making the trade if it came down to it, but the waiting and anticipation had her stomach in knots. She hoped no one could tell. The three of them were smiling as they rounded the house and walked into a wonderland lit up by beautiful hanging lanterns and the moon. The decorations were stunning, but Sophia was starting to realize not to expect anything less than extraordinary from Richard Vega. An elevated stage overlooked the party area behind the house while a mini-orchestra was seated on its beautifully stained wood. A canopy covered half the stage while gold and silver lanterns drooped from the rafters. The party area stretched far and wide with pockets of white chairs and alternating gold and silver tables. Waiters and waitresses walked around with platters filled with hors d'oeuvres while two long buffet tables draped in sheer cloth stood in the middle. Everything was white, gold or silver. It was all beautiful and yet oddly reminiscent of her senior prom.

Men and women wearing cocktail attire were already milling around, eating finger foods and making small talk. When Braydon had said it was the event of the year, she could see he wasn't the only person who held that as truth. Culpepper natives had more than stepped up in their dressed-for-the-best attire.

"Glad you could make it," Richard greeted, after catching their eye while talking to one of the waiters. A few of the attendants moved closer to him as she made her way over. Richard really was like a modern-day prince in Culpepper—everyone seemed to gravitate toward him. "I trust the walk here was pleasant?" he asked with a winning smile. The man sure worked well under pressure.

"It was a breeze," Sophia answered. She tried to mimic his smile.

Richard had already been briefed about the night's plans. All he had to do was pretend that he knew nothing about what was going on. Captain Westin had even gone as far as to tell the man not to mention any of Nathanial's victims, including Lisa.

"If anyone comes up to you and asks about any of them, change the subject," he'd said to all of them. "We don't need a bunch of civilians running around worried or trying to play cop. We'll play ignorant until we finally get him." It had been a hard pill to swallow for Richard, especially given the fact that most everyone would wonder why Lisa wasn't at his side—especially at an event she had originally planned—but he had promised his lips would remain sealed.

"I'm glad." Richard extended his arms in a sweeping gesture. "Welcome to the seventh annual Culpepper Fund-raiser. Feel free to eat, dance and meet some wonderful people." The second part sounded rehearsed, Sophia thought, but Richard had been the host for seven years running. It was natural to him by now. He left to mingle with a new wave of partygoers while Sophia and Cara followed Braydon to the buffet tables. Sophia's nerves had pushed her appetite to the back burner but she didn't mind taking a glass of champagne that was offered to her by a floating waitress.

"You okay there, Miss Hardwick?" Braydon asked with a big smile. It was only for appearance's sake—the concern was sewn into each word.

"Never better," she lied before tipping her glass back for a long drink. It was smooth and delicious.

"Remember, you need to try and keep a low profile here," Braydon reminded her for the umpteenth time. It was his protective side coming out. A part of him didn't want Nathanial to see her, but that was the whole reason she was there in the first place.

"Don't worry," she said in what she hoped was an even voice. "Just wanted to get my feet a little wet is all."

Cara smiled and said, "I like the way you think." She grabbed a glass and the two clinked them together.

"Women," Braydon mumbled.

By the time eight o'clock rolled around, the party was

in full swing. Being the outsider she was, Sophia didn't recognize anyone minus a few cops, and they made sure to mingle away from the three of them. Braydon, however, was a different story. Every time he seemed to turn around there was someone ready to congratulate him on the promotion or talk football scores or share a few pieces of gossip with him. Sophia's favorite local who stopped to chat was an elderly woman named Ms. Perry. She had her flirt turned on high and occasionally would reach up to pinch Braydon's cheeks after he said something that she deemed adorable.

"I'm about to make my speech," Richard said after Perry hobbled off to find another glass of champagne. "But first, can I have a moment alone with Sophia?" He directed the question to Braydon. It annoyed her immensely yet felt flattering in a way, as if Richard was asking her man if he could have the next dance.

"Stay inside the party and in my sight line," Braydon said after a thoughtful pause, clearly weighing the pros and cons. It didn't offend Richard in the least. He agreed and the two of them walked as far back from the party as Braydon would be comfortable with.

Sophia looked expectantly at the man her sister loved. He was handsome in his suit but she found herself comparing him to the detective like she had the first day she'd met both men. They each were dressed right for the occasion but Sophia thought they looked worlds apart. Richard was the authentic businessman—dressed to make money and attract clients. He looked handsome but not necessarily mouthwatering good-looking. Braydon on the other hand was reminiscent of a Bond character—suave and sexy with an overpowering sense of confidence. His suit let the world know he was ready to party but equally ready for any action that might come his way. She knew his gun was at his side beneath his blazer—also ready for a potential fray.

"How are you holding up?" Richard asked when they were out of hearing distance from the closest group of partiers.

"Honestly? I hate this, but I'm trying to stay hopeful. What about you?"

"It's been hell," he admitted. "I've been asked where Lisa is a dozen times. I keep coming up with more lies and excuses to field each question." He rubbed at his eyes. He suddenly looked years older than his thirty-four. "I just want her home." Sophia couldn't help it— she wrapped Richard into a quick embrace.

"I know what you mean." He returned the hug. It was brief but it was the most goodwill she had ever shown the man. "I never said it, but thank you for all that you've done trying to find her. I know I haven't been the best sister about your relationship, but I didn't know you before." She quirked the corner of her lip up into a little smile. "I know it doesn't mean much right now, but you two have my full blessing." Richard's face broke out into the first genuine smile she had seen from him.

"Thank you, Sophia. That means a lot to me…and Lisa. I just hope everything goes well tonight. That Lisa *and* you stay safe."

They made their way back into the midst of the party relatively unnoticed but it was like all of the men's pocketbooks had a Richard Vega radar that blipped quite loudly when he was in close proximity. The whole "keep a low profile" idea had become just that—an idea. One that Sophia was having a hard time practicing, through no fault of her own. There was only so much she could do about her revealing dress. When the men around Richard weren't transfixed on the rich man, they were ogling her chest and legs. She was about to tell the nearest older man where her eyes were located when a sickening feeling crawled through her.

Without looking, she knew Nathanial was out there now, watching. She could feel it. Whether he was out in the trees that stood on each side of Richard's house or hiding amongst the hundreds of people that made up the crowd, a very daring move if true, he was somewhere out there, waiting for her to come forward. Waiting for her to make the trade.

An older man with a thick mustache and flowing gut led the crowd that halted Sophia and Richard as he made a beeline for the host's attention. He gave Sophia a small nod before effectively cutting her off from the rich man. His back became a barrier of expensive satin. She looked around the crowd and noticed more men dressed in meticulously pressed suits eyeing Richard as if he was a juicy steak and they were the rabid dogs. Maybe he was the one who needed police protection.

Among the ones near the buffet tables were Braydon and Cara. She wondered if they'd even moved while she had gone to talk to Richard. They were staring at her— Braydon with a look that conveyed worry with a touch of something else and Cara with an approving smile. Sure a killer had given Sophia a dress, but that didn't mean it wasn't one heck of a great dress.

"You and Richard seem to be quite close," Lynda the receptionist said by way of greeting before Sophia could walk back to her group. She wore a dress that didn't hide any of her assets. It dipped low, had no back and rose up to the middle of her thighs as she walked. Sophia didn't have room to judge, but at the same time she had been told to wear *her* dress. Lynda had poured herself into her slinky number on her own accord. Sophia wouldn't have been so critical had the woman not accessorized her outfit with an outright sneer.

"We just needed a moment away from everyone," she explained, trying not to stare at the cleavage that somehow was pushed up so high, it almost hit the woman's neck. She glanced down at her own and was relieved to see it wasn't as out there. "We needed some alone time to talk about a few things. Talk about Lisa." Lynda was one of the few who knew Lisa had been kidnapped because she worked at the station. She shouldn't have been surprised that the two of them were talking.

"How nice for you two." Lynda didn't dial down the accusatory tone that she was currently carrying; the implications of something romantic or sexual going on between Sophia and the party's host weren't missed. "So I heard that you stayed here last night. I guess Braydon's place wasn't to your liking, huh?" She plucked the toothpick from her drink and sucked the olive off it. It wasn't the classiest thing Sophia had seen, but she was betting Lynda was touching tipsy. "It's a shame, you know. Braydon is *all* kinds of fun."

Sophia wanted the conversation to end fast. There was no time to sit around playing catty. Lynda wasn't even trying to hide her jealousy that Braydon and Sophia had been getting close. And she didn't even know about last night. They weren't in high school and, quite frankly, she didn't have the patience for this. However, she couldn't deny that at the same time, she wanted to stake her claim on the man Lynda had once dated.

"Oh, on the contrary, I am quite fond of Detective Thatcher." She lowered her voice and wiggled her eyebrows. "As for how fun he is, I'm pretty sure if last night was any indication, I'll definitely have to agree with you there." Lynda's mouth dropped open—the half-eaten olive showing. Sophia stopped the look of disgust from covering her features. "Now, if you'll excuse me." She didn't wait for whatever comment was about to spring from the other woman's bright-red lips. "Richard said he is about to make an important announcement and I want to get a front-row view." This did nothing to perk up the receptionist. Her whole body seemed taut with shock and jealousy. She took her leave of the woman and made her way through the crowd to the detective and officer, looking back once to see Lynda staring after.

"What was *that* about?" Cara asked, confusing Braydon.

"Oh, you know, just fun girl talk." She didn't hide the sarcasm. "Why don't we go get us a front-row spot?" They nodded and Braydon took Sophia's hand, leading her through the crowd, Cara and her black cocktail dress in their wake. The olive-eating, jealous Lynda followed, stopping behind them as they made their way to the front of the stage. Cara looked between the two women before giving Sophia a grin and rolling her eyes. It seemed that she wasn't the only one who disliked the scantily clad woman.

"What did Richard have to say?" Braydon asked, oblivious to the silent conversation going on behind his back, but she didn't get a chance to answer. Richard took his place on the stage, which was elevated two or three feet off the ground, and cleared his throat. The sound was surprisingly loud and clear—it cut through the chatter of the crowd and brought silence to the party of people.

"If you would please gather around." He motioned to the empty space on both sides of their group. Braydon hadn't let go of Sophia's hand—it warmed her skin and helped bring back her original calm. His brow was furrowed and his eyes went right through Richard. The man of the hour smiled and turned his focus to the rapt crowd. "First off, let me begin by saying a warm thank-you for attending this year's fund-raising event. Without good people like you in the world, such things could not exist. So, let's take a drink for all of those in attendance." He raised his glass and brought it to his lips. Most of the crowd followed his actions. Richard smiled after his sip, though it was more like a lengthy swallow, and continued. "Second, thank you for any and all donations and purchases you may make tonight. This fund-raiser has become a tradition that helps out organizations and charities throughout Culpepper. Everything earned here tonight will only help further the town's progress and success. Now, speaking of traditions, I'd like to sidestep another one this year—the welcome speech's length. Most of you can recall last year's record half-hour address and I'm sorry about that. I do believe I had a bit too much champagne at that point." He paused for laughter. It came easily. "Tonight I'd like to keep it short and sweet and say welcome to the seventh annual Culpepper Fund-raiser! As always the auction will start at eight-thirty. Cheers!" The crowd shouted back with excitement and took another celebratory swig of alcohol alongside their host.

Sophia finished off her second glass and smiled at Richard. She was proud of her sister for not listening to her when she'd implied that he was nothing more than a rich jerk. *That* was a label that would remain a secret between the sisters. Richard caught her eye and gave a small nod.

"You have got to be kidding me. I think it's time to take a smoke break," Lynda said, all but huffing as she turned on her heel.

"What's her problem?" Braydon asked, though he didn't seem much invested in whatever the answer would be.

His eyes scanned the faces of each and every partygoer he could see.

"She has some issues with my *friendship* with a certain detective. Apparently she used to be really good *friends* with him." Sophia could have laughed at how Braydon's entire demeanor stiffened. He shot a dirty look at Cara who had just found her nails to be fascinating. It looked as though he hadn't been prepared for her to know about his past relationship.

"That was a long time ago," he defended. "I ended it. That woman has more than one screw loose."

Sophia smiled at the red that filled the detective's cheeks. It was the first time she'd seen him blush. The result was oddly charming. He tried to put together an explanation, though he didn't owe her one. She placed a hand on his chest to stop him.

"Calm down, Detective. I told her being friends with you was *a lot* of fun." Cara laughed out loud and Sophia couldn't help but join her. It was nice to laugh. It helped ease her nerves, if only for a moment.

The music picked back up as the first organization prepared for their auction time. If the whole event hadn't been a cover to draw out Nathanial, Sophia would have liked to watch the bidding. When she had first come to Culpepper, she had disliked the small town and its residents, favoring the city. However, the more she was around them, the more fascinating she found the charming place. Minus the obvious bad seed named Nathanial Williams. They all knew each other—they were all connected somehow. Standing between Braydon and Cara, she felt like even she was a part of that connection. She wondered how it would feel if Lisa was here, safe and sound, while Nathanial was long gone.

She didn't get a chance to think about it too much,

though, because just as they were about to get situated in the crowd to watch the first auction, a scream tore through the night air. Like the carrying voice of Richard, its effect on the crowd was instantaneous. The band stopped playing while everyone looked in the direction of the nearest tree line looming ominously behind the boundaries of the party. Another scream sounded, this time with words attached.

"He's here!"

Chapter Eighteen

Lynda came crashing out of the trees and into the haven of lights created by the lanterns that boxed in the party. Her face was fear stricken. "I saw him! He's in there!" That didn't mean much to most of the fund-raiser's guests, but it sure got every cop in the crowd moving as one in the direction Lynda was pointing. Braydon hesitated for a moment before springing to action.

"Sophia, you stay here or so help me—"

"Go!" She shooed him. "Get Lisa!"

Braydon nodded, brought out the gun from under his jacket and ran full tilt after the officers who poured into the woods. Cara, tasked with sticking to Sophia's side no matter the occasion, grabbed the crook of her arm while Richard's assistant Jordan ran to the microphone and tried to calm everyone down. Richard had disappeared, no doubt going after Nathanial, too. Sophia and Cara hurried to the shaking shell that was Lynda.

"I just wanted to smoke a cigarette," she said as they approached, looking wildly between them. "I didn't want to piss anyone off so I took a walk. He was just standing there with a—a big needle in his hand." Fresh tears rolled down her cheeks.

"Was there a woman with him?" Sophia asked. "Was Lisa with him?"

"I don't know." Her voice shook. "I'm sorry. I saw him and just freaked." Sophia's stomach fell. Was Lisa not with him after all? Did this mean that the trade had been a trick? Was Lisa even alive still?

"Do you think Richard would mind if we went inside to sit down?" Lynda asked. "It's too *exposed* out here."

"That's actually a good idea," Cara agreed, eyeing the tree line.

"But—" Sophia started to argue. Cara wasn't having it.

"We'll stay in the living room," she said, already moving with Lynda toward the giant house. "Plus, I have my gun." She pulled it from the purse she had been toting. Sophia relented but looked back, hoping Braydon was okay.

The three of them wove through the crowd to the door that led from the stage into the back of the living area. Jordan eyed them warily from the mic but when he recognized them he waved his approval to go inside. Not that Cara would have stopped had he said no. It was the first time Sophia had seen her in full cop mode. She made a mental note to never mess with the woman.

This was a part of the house Sophia had never seen, sticking to the kitchen, study and second floor during her stay. It was just as opulent and clean as Richard's office a hallway over and, even though she wasn't a fan of animal prints and white as a decor combination, it seemed to work for the space. Lynda held the door open for them but didn't stop once it was shut.

"I need some water," she said, pointing toward the kitchen.

"We need to stay in here," Cara said. The view to the party was uninhibited thanks to floor-to-ceiling windows that lined the wall. "I'd feel more comfortable if we could see everyone."

Lynda gave Cara a slap on the arm. "Come on, Cara, it's only a room away," she tried.

Cara touched the spot Lynda had hit.

"Watch it," she complained, "that hurt."

"Sorry, it must have been my ring. Can I go get some water now?"

Cara sighed but nodded. Sophia wanted to stay by the window but knew she wouldn't be allowed to do so alone. She followed the cop with her own sigh. They hadn't made it more than a few steps into the kitchen before Cara stopped suddenly.

"You aren't wearing any rings" was all she could say before she lost her balance and pitched backward. Sophia tried to keep the woman upright but she was a good few inches taller and heavier. All she could do was slow the fall. "Cara?" she shrieked, hitting the ground with the woman on top of her. "Cara?" The officer was unconscious. Confusion surfaced before Cara's last words registered. Sophia looked at Lynda. She was smirking.

"That took *forever* to work." Lynda held a small syringe and needle up for her to see. "I honestly didn't think she'd ever pass out."

Sophia's face contorted into a mask of rage. "Why?" she asked.

"Why? Well, because you wore the dress. That means you want to trade." She held out the used syringe. "Wasn't that the plan, Nate?"

Sophia felt sick as Nathanial walked around the corner and took the syringe. He wore a black suit with a red button-down shirt that almost matched his hair. His tie was as white as the grin he was currently wearing.

"That's right." He pulled out a bag from his suit pocket

and switched out the used syringe for a new one. Sophia watched in muted horror as Lynda pushed her hair out of the way and let Nathanial inject her with it. "Remember, you might want to lay down. As everyone in the room can tell you, this works rather fast."

Lynda nodded and sat down on the hardwood.

"Good luck with your vengeance," she told him with what Sophia only could describe as a flirtatious smile. "Let me know if you ever want to do this again."

Nathanial didn't respond but instead turned his attention to Sophia. Lynda slumped against the wall and fell the rest of the way to the floor. Her dress was even more unflattering in its rumpled state.

"You weren't in the woods," Sophia stammered, meeting the cold, dark eyes of "Terrance" Williams. "She lied for you."

He held up his index finger and wiggled it back and forth. "She didn't lie for me, Sophia. She lied for money," he corrected. "There is a difference." He came closer and grabbed the gun that had fallen away from Cara's hand. Instant fear seized hold of her chest, but he held out his other hand for her. "Now, let's go see your sister."

Sophia felt bad for pushing Cara off her, but she did it as gently as she could manage from beneath the woman. This time Nathanial didn't tell her to inject the drug into her veins. Instead, he looped his arm through hers and guided her upstairs before stopping just outside the farthest room from the landing—three doors down from the room she had been staying in. Sophia's heart pounded in her chest. She gave the killer a questioning look.

"The deal was you get to say goodbye, remember?" He detached her arm from his before producing another, smaller syringe from his jacket. How much more of that stuff had he made? He opened the door but held her wrist firmly.

The world melted away in a rush of relief so strong that it brought tears to Sophia's eyes. Sitting up on the bed was Lisa and, even though her arms and legs were tied and a piece of cloth was stuffed in her mouth, Sophia couldn't help but smile. She was alive. It was a fact that overpowered her with a rush of courage. In one swift movement she turned and kicked Nathanial hard in the groin. He doubled over and the gun dropped from his hand. She lunged after it, scooping it up just as he pulled her to him. He pushed a needle into her skin at the same moment she pulled the trigger.

A loud bang sounded. Nathanial roared in anger and threw her against the ground. The gun fell from her hands and skidded across the floor and under the bed. Sophia knew she didn't have long. She looked up at her sister. They locked eyes and for the first time in a long while Sophia felt content.

"I love you," she said.

Then the darkness came.

Chapter Nineteen

"This is too easy," Braydon said, stopping to catch his breath. His gun was raised in front of him.

"What?" Richard had been running next to him, undeterred by the fact that he had no weapon to defend himself. The rest of the woods were swarming with cops, yet no one had yelled back that they had made contact or even seen Nathanial or Lisa.

"This was too easy," he said again, already starting to turn around. "I think he's at the party." Richard didn't question him as the detective backtracked, running harder than before. He followed with surprising speed.

The crowd hadn't moved, thanks to Jordan spouting some nonsense on the microphone, but when they saw Braydon run out with his gun raised and their host right behind everything got loud. He didn't care—his focus had narrowed as it swept across the clumps of people.

Sophia and Cara were nowhere to be seen.

"Jordan!" Richard yelled after they fought their way to the stage. "Have you seen Sophia and Officer Whitfield?"

Jordan's mouth was slightly agape as he looked between his rumpled boss and the gun-wielding detective. He pointed to the back door without a word.

"Stay behind me," Braydon growled out of professional reflex. He didn't care about anyone other than Sophia right now. He threw open the door and for the second time in a handful of minutes, felt the sharp stab of dread. Cara and Lynda were laid out on the floor, unconscious, and Sophia was nowhere in sight.

"Call this in," Braydon snapped, not bothering to look back at Richard as he stepped over the two women. His gun remained raised and he quickly searched the bottom floor. He entered each room with his heart in his throat and white-hot anger in his eyes.

"Braydon," Richard called out after his first-floor search ended. He ran back to meet the man at the stairs. "Something fell upstairs." From somewhere Richard had produced his own handgun and started to lead the way. When they reached the top they paused, listening. A second later there was a loud *thud* at the end of the hall. Braydon rushed forward, waiting only until Richard got on the other side of the door, and flung it open.

On the floor next to the bed was Lisa Hardwick. As Richard cried out and ran over to her, Braydon knew he should be happy that they had finally found her, but he couldn't, knowing what the cost had been. Richard removed the cloth from her mouth. That's when Braydon noticed a dark red stain against the hardwood.

"He'll take her to the dock!" she rasped out as soon as her mouth was free.

"She's alive?" he had to ask once he realized what he was looking at was blood.

"Yes, he drugged her and took off after she shot him."

"She shot him?" Richard asked, working on the ties around Lisa's legs.

Braydon heard her say yes but was already out of the room and running down the stairs. *This is it,* he thought, *this is where it ends.*

SOPHIA COULD HEAR the soft lull of water nearby. It pushed against the hard surface beneath her, causing a swaying rhythm. Unlike the last time she had been injected with Nathanial's homemade drug, she wasn't lost in a haze when she came to. It was easier this time around, she thought.

"I'm glad you could join me," said a voice to her side. Everything that had happened came back in a rush. She sat up straight and flinched away from him. Before she could move an inch, Nathanial pulled her toward him and looped his arm around her shoulder. His grip was firm. His eyes were crazed.

"What's happening?" she asked, disoriented by the change in her surroundings.

"What's happening?" he repeated. An eruption of laughter escaped his throat as he turned to look her in the eyes. In the moonlight his face looked more twisted than it had in the basement of the hospital. Darker shadows played across his features while his skin had a pale sheen of sweat covering it, plastering his hair and clothes to his body. His jacket was missing and there was a dark red stain growing on his side. It seeped through the light red of his shirt.

"I shot you," she said with a start, remembering pulling the trigger. She hadn't realized it actually hit him.

"You sure did." He brought his other hand up and wagged his finger at her. She didn't mind the gesture but she did mind the gun in his grip. "It wasn't very nice, you know? I had to speed up my entire plan."

"Speed up?"

He skimmed over that question and motioned around them.

"This is where it all started, Sophia Hardwick." They were sitting on the edge of the dock, water slapping against the wood. In front of them was an expansive body of water closed in by a line of trees in the distance. Sophia craned her head around to see a house a hundred or so yards behind them. She turned back to face the water.

Nathanial's words sunk in.

"This is where Amelia was killed."

"Bingo!" Nathanial said. "Though technically they found her body over there off to the side." He pointed back to the beginning of the dock. She spotted a car parked in front of the house. She bet that it was his.

"You want to kill me where she was killed."

He nodded. "Was there really any other place to do it?"

Sophia's stomach turned to ice. "Will my death really help you move on?"

Nathanial laughed again before stopping to wince. "I don't expect it will. Then again, I don't expect to live much longer, either. Your lack of aim managed to do more damage than I would have liked." He looked down at the bullet wound. "It's almost poetic that Braydon won't have the satisfaction of killing me, just like he didn't have the satisfaction of killing my brother." He moved his wrist to check his watch. "He should be here soon."

"How do you know?"

He shrugged, all nonchalant. "I imagine your sister has told him by now. That is, if they even found her." He cursed beneath his breath, wincing again. "I may have been too clever about all of this."

"Why do any of it?" she asked. "Why go through all of this?"

"Because Braydon has to pay for Terrance's death," he growled, his composure slipping. "He has to pay for what he did to my family. After my folks left town, they were never the same. Dad took to drinking and dropped dead and Mom…she held on as long as she could. I tried to help her, but—" He paused before lowering his voice. "But I wasn't enough for her." He hung his head like a disappointed child. Sophia dared not move. The man had clearly lost what little sanity he once had.

"Is that when you decided to come back to Culpepper?" If she was going to die, she at least wanted to know.

"Yes…and no. A part of me always thought about coming back."

"Is that why you changed your name?"

He tensed. "Mother told me the name change would make her happy." His head drooped lower. She thought he was going to pass out but he straightened up after a moment. "It didn't. So, I went back to school." It sounded like Nathanial wasn't the only unstable member of his family. To ask a child to rename himself after his deceased sibling was just not right. The air grew thick with silence. Sophia hoped to every god out there that Nathanial would either fall unconscious from blood loss or just outright die. His story may have been sad but that was no excuse for all he had done. However, she had to ask at least one more question.

"Were you the one who got Lisa to go to the Dolphin Lot?" Sophia could tell the pain he was feeling had worsened. His face was pinched when he answered.

"Guilty." He smiled again, as if he was proud of what he'd done.

"What did you say to get her to meet you?"

"I told a few fibs. I said I was about to purchase the lot and was interested in selling some of it to her for her planning business, but first I wanted her to come check out the area to see if she'd even be interested."

"And she just agreed, without telling anyone?"

He shrugged. "I asked her to keep it a secret because

all the paperwork wasn't done yet. She agreed because she was excited. When we met, I told her I planned on killing her. She tried to run, I grabbed her, then took her. It was easy as pie." Sophia felt nauseous. Nathanial spoke as though Lisa was just a pawn in a horrible and twisted game of chess. He may have been brilliant at his job but he was so far off base when it came to basic humanity.

"And what about Trixie? Amanda? Why did you pick them? What was the point?"

"Trixie was a happy accident. I was setting up my spot to view Braydon discovering Lisa's body in the car, that is before I was ready to stage her, when she came jogging by. She saw the car and I had no choice but to keep her quiet. Plus, it worked out wonderfully. I was able to see Braydon's feelings for you." At this he grinned. "Amanda would have been fine had she not followed my car out here when I came to check on everything. I only started talking to her to get information about the land. I took her to Lynda's so she could serve as your message later." He turned and winked. "It's amazing how easy it was to sway that woman to help me. It started as a joke over some drinks at the bar then all it took to make it a reality was the promise of money."

Sophia was about to ask how much money Lynda had been promised when Nathanial let go of her shoulders. He put his hand to his wound, then held it up to the moonlight. Dark red dripped from his fingers.

"Maybe Braydon isn't as fast as I need him to be right now. I guess it's time for you to die, Miss Hardwick. I truly am sorry that he won't be able to see you take your last breath." He struggled to stand and Sophia went with the only option she had left. She lifted up into a crouch and threw all her weight into the man. Startled, Nathanial pulled the trigger before the two of them toppled over the edge of the dock and into the water.

Sophia's adrenaline surged as they hit the cold water, going under in a tangle of limbs. For a man who was so keen on dying, Nathanial thrashed around, fighting to break away from her grip. Though, Sophia wasn't budging. She wasn't sure but she thought she had heard the *thunk* of the gun hitting the dock. Nathanial had already made it crystal clear that he wanted Sophia dead. If he got to the gun, he *would* kill her.

Sophia's plan quickly backfired. Nathanial grabbed a fistful of her hair as his feet found the bottom of the bay. He pushed her farther underwater, using his other hand to press her back down. He didn't need the gun to kill her now. He was going to drown her. She thrashed around, heart slamming against her rib cage. She used her nails to claw at his hands and, when he didn't let up, she remembered the bullet wound. With the last of her energy, she threw her hand out and jabbed her fingers into the wound. Even underwater she heard him yell. He let go and she scrambled to the surface.

"You little bitch!" he howled, the water coming up to his chin. Sophia didn't wait to hear what he said next. She swam around the dock until her feet hit the muddy ground. The air should have chilled her wet body but she was still in the throes of an adrenaline high. She ran out of the water as fast as she could.

"Stop, or I'll shoot!" Nathanial yelled. She whipped around to see him standing on the dock. He picked up the gun and held it firm in his hand. Sophia's shoulder burned, her throat ached, and more than anything she wanted to kiss Braydon Thatcher goodbye. "Before you die, I want you to know that I may have killed you but it's still his fault." He sneered as he said it.

"It's not Braydon's fault!" she snapped. "It wasn't his fault eleven years ago and it isn't his fault now!" She stumbled to the side, suddenly feeling faint. Her adrenaline must have run out. "When you kill me, Nathanial Williams, I want you to remember that it was your fault."

Sophia fell to her knees just as the gunshot rang through the night. She waited for the lights to turn off—to be the victim of darkness that would never let up. She waited for death but it didn't come. Instead Nathanial fell backward into the water, a bullet piercing his forehead. She turned around, confused, to see Braydon lower his gun. He was the most beautiful man she had ever seen.

"Good shot," she greeted, but he didn't smile back at her. The detective grabbed his phone and dialed a number—his brow creased, his lips downturned in a frown. *What a weird time to make a phone call,* she thought fleetingly.

"What's the status on the ambulance?" he barked into his phone, dropping down beside her. He still wouldn't meet her eyes.

"He doesn't need an ambulance, Braydon," she said, looking toward the dock. "Nathanial's dead." Braydon ignored what she said as if he couldn't hear her. Instead he yelled more into the phone before flinging it into the dirt.

"Sophia, I need you to stay awake, okay?" he said. It sounded farther away than it should have with him being so close. She was confused but nodded all the same. She trusted Braydon. She felt safe with him. He put his hand above her chest. It brought on an unexpected, terrible pain. She looked down to see what he had done, ready to fuss at him.

"Oh," she managed.

Apparently, Sophia hadn't been the only one to get a lucky shot in. It looked like Nathanial might have got his wish after all.

Chapter Twenty

The world was bright, warm and horizontal. Sophia opened her eyes to the buzz of fluorescent lights and the face of a woman with identical green eyes.

Lisa was perched on the side of the bed, smiling down at her little sister. There were dark purple bruises that lined the left side of her face and a scab across her bottom lip. Even though her face was devoid of makeup, Sophia couldn't help but be proud of how beautiful Lisa was.

"Your eye," Sophia said, jumping to the most relevant thing. She smacked her lips together—her mouth was unbearably dry. Lisa read her mind and produced a cup of water with a straw.

"Don't worry about this," Lisa said. "Out of everyone Nathanial hurt, I'm the one with the least damage." Sophia was glad to hear that. She pulled on the straw until her cracked lips felt smooth. Lisa took the cup when she was done.

"I'm glad you're alive," Sophia said. Her throat felt better, but her head felt sluggish. "I can't count how many times I almost lost hope that I'd ever see you again."

"I knew you wouldn't give up. You're too darn stubborn." She laughed but then all humor disappeared.

"I was afraid I'd never see *you* again." Lisa's brow

furrowed and her eyes began to water. "Sugar, you were shot. If Braydon hadn't gotten to you in time…"

Sophia reached up and grabbed her hand, squeezed it and smiled.

"But he did and I'm okay." She paused. Maybe she couldn't claim that, considering she'd woken up in the hospital. "I am okay, right?" Lisa's seriousness lessened. She nodded and smiled. Sophia realized how much she had missed the image.

"Yes, you are. Apparently you're *so* stubborn that you won't let things like bullets in the shoulder stop you." She sobered. "You've only been here for a few hours. They had trouble getting all of the bullet bits out, and they were nervous about how much of Nathanial's drug you had been given in such a short amount of time, but in the end the doctor gave you the okay." She reached forward and lightly touched the large bandage that was over the front of her shoulder. "It'll scar, though." Sophia frowned, thinking of Amanda's stomach. Nathanial had branded her without a care in the world.

"Nathanial is dead," she stated with some venom. Again Lisa nodded, her long hair slipping from her ponytail at the movement.

"Yes, he is."

Sophia also liked the sound of that.

"Braydon had to go back to the police station to talk with the captain and deal with paperwork because of it."

Sophia's heart did a little flutter at the mention of the detective. She didn't want to admit it, but when she found that Braydon hadn't been in the room, her stomach had dropped. Nathanial's reign of terror was over. Lisa had been found. The case of the missing Culpepper women was solved. Their romance had started in the heat of extreme circumstances and now that the danger had passed, Sophia wondered where that left them.

Lisa put her thumb between Sophia's eyebrows and pushed down.

"Stop your worrying," she ordered. "You've had enough troubles this past week to deal with. Try to relax, okay?" She moved her hand away and her brilliant smile returned. "And just to let you know, I basically had to kick Braydon out after the captain called him."

"Why?" Sophia tried to keep her voice from showing how much she cared about the man's presence. Although, she was sure Lisa had already picked up on the fact that her little sister was pining for him.

"He wanted to make sure you were okay. He didn't even leave the hospital until you were out of surgery." She winked. "He was stuck to your side like glue." Sophia couldn't stop the smile that crept across her lips. Lisa's grew, too. "I thought there might be something there."

They stayed in a giddy bubble of happiness for a moment before Sophia had to start asking questions about what had happened. Lisa must have realized it was coming. Her smile faded and she pushed her shoulders back, readying for the inquiries.

"What happened?" Sophia started. It was an umbrella question that would lead to all of the answers she wanted.

The Saturday night before Sophia's birthday party, Lisa had received a call from a man she now knew was Nathanial, claiming he was about to purchase Dolphin Lot. Lisa hadn't known the history behind the Alcaster property but she did know that it was a beautiful space and that it was undeveloped. The man went on to say that after he purchased it, he wanted Details to be able to use one of the acres as an event space, but he wanted Lisa to see the lot with him first.

"I jumped at that," Lisa said. "An entire acre of Dolphin Lot could be used for great outdoor parties and weddings. It would double my client base alone. When he asked me to keep it a secret until everything was finalized, I thought it was a small price to pay for such an amazing opportunity. He wanted to meet that Monday but I told him I had my sister's birthday to attend. So, I offered to meet him Sunday morning before I left instead." Lisa grabbed her hand. "If I hadn't done that…" She became quiet. Sophia waited, not wanting to push the woman. "I met him on the road. He grabbed me, threw me into his car and then drugged me. I woke up in Lynda Meyer's enclosed garage."

Sophia's jaw hardened. "I can't believe she helped him." Having Lynda, a woman who worked for the police department, be the variable no one had expected, had been a smart move. She knew the case's progress and where Sophia had been at all times. Not to mention, no one had suspected her.

"After Nathanial took Amanda out, Lynda finally showed herself. She told me that it was nothing personal—Nathanial had just given her a lot of money. He promised her that no one would ever know she had helped him."

"Then why did she let us see that she was in on it? Didn't she know that you and Cara would tell everyone about her?"

"She probably thought you were as good as dead." Lisa paused, not liking those words. "And apparently Nathanial promised that he had left me dead in the upstairs room at Richard's and also would finish off any other loose ends, which I assume meant Cara. Lynda woke up an hour ago in handcuffs." Sophia couldn't deny that seeing Lynda in handcuffs would make her happy.

"I still can't believe any of this happened," Sophia breathed. Lisa had gone missing a week ago but it felt like years.

"I can't believe you shot Nathanial at Richard's," she admonished. "What if he had gotten a hold of the gun and killed you right then and there?"

"We both know he wouldn't have done that. He wanted Braydon to see me die for his big finale or, at the very least, kill me on the stage of his choice."

Lisa frowned. "I'm just glad Braydon showed up in time."

"Me, too."

Silence filled the room again. This time it was loaded. Lisa's eyes began to water again.

"Sophia…" she began, looking down at their clasped hands. "Richard told me what you did at the hospital, taking the syringe when you could have run. Then volunteering to turn yourself over to him…" She met Sophia's gaze. Her eyes were shining green orbs. "You saved me, Sophia. No one else did. It was you. I—I just don't know how to repay you for what you did." Sophia smiled at her sister's emotional gush.

"It isn't a debt, Lisa," she said. "You don't owe me anything because I'm your sister and I love you. So, don't cry because you know it makes me uncomfortable." Lisa laughed but nodded, wiping under her eyes. "Now, is there anything else I missed?"

"Actually, there is." Lisa composed herself enough to smile wide. She held up her left hand. A beautiful diamond graced her ring finger. Sophia copied the smile. "He said he's been holding on to it for a while, waiting for the perfect moment. After everything that happened, he said he didn't want to wait anymore. Plus, I heard *someone* gave him their blessing."

"It's beautiful," Sophia said honestly.

"I could care less about the actual ring. It's the man who makes me happy. There's only one problem, though."

Sophia raised her eyebrow. "What's that?"

"Since I practically live at Richard's anyway, it only makes sense to sell my house. But that can be such a lengthy, unpleasant process, especially when dealing with strangers. If there was someone who I *knew* was interested it would make everything easier. Someone who, perhaps, wouldn't mind taking care of all of my pillows." Lisa winked. "I'd even consider renting it out if that fit the person's needs better." Sophia understood the meaning her sister was pushing. Although she had an apartment and job back in the city, she couldn't deny that Culpepper and one very handsome detective had changed what she thought of as "home."

"Are you sure she'll like this?" Braydon looked around his living room, skeptical of the brightly colored streamers that hung from each corner. The contrast between the purples, blues and pinks of the party decorations and the oak wood and leather was an odd combination to see. Cara stood with her hands on her hips and did a 360-degree turn. She nodded her approval.

"I think she'll love it, especially considering she spent her actual birthday thinking her sister didn't care enough to show up. What with her being kidnapped and all," Cara said. "That woman deserves a little party."

Braydon nodded, he couldn't have agreed more.

A week had passed since Braydon had killed Nathanial Williams, ending the sick cycle of a terrible, violent past. In a way he felt as if he had finally found justice for Amelia, killing "Terrance" before he had a chance to hurt anyone else. Though, he knew he couldn't take all of the credit.

Nathanial hadn't bet on Sophia fighting back. She had thrown everything at the man, wounding him and giving Braydon enough time to get to the dock and finish the job. In a way, Sophia had saved her own life. Culpepper had since returned to normal while those affected slowly started to heal.

Cara had woken up from Nathanial's drug, groggy but unharmed and had personally handcuffed Lynda to her hospital bed before the receptionist had awoken. Lynda was facing charges that would put her away for a long, long time. The money that had been deposited in her bank account by Nathanial had been extracted and used to pay for Trixie Martin's and James Murphy's funerals. Instead of finally getting rid of the Dolphin Lot and moving far away, Marina Alcaster had turned the rights over to her daughter who had decided she wanted to build and run a small bed-and-breakfast on the land nearest the water. She had then sold two acres of the land to Lisa, who had paid for it with her own money. Lisa had told him that before Sophia had been discharged from the hospital, Amanda had stopped by her room and relieved the guilt that had been clouding her mind.

"You didn't physically do this to me, so I expect you to not feel bad about it," she had said after showing the puckered marks that spelled out Sophia's name across her stomach. Amanda even went as far as to joke, "I'm just glad you don't have a longer name."

Lisa also let it slip that Sophia had finally called their mother and the three of them were slowly trying to repair their relationship. It reminded Braydon that he needed to give his own parents a call. At the end of the long story they promised to visit him soon.

Richard had also made a town-wide announcement that the annual Culpepper Fund-raiser would make another visit within the next three months since it had been shut down before any of the auctions started. There would also be an addition of a new program that promoted mental health awareness and was aimed at working with those with issues to help get them the attention they needed. He also announced his engagement, inviting everyone in town to the wedding at the end of the year. Braydon had no doubt in his mind that it would be one of the most extravagant ceremonies he would ever see.

Braydon and Tom had spent the majority of the week completing paperwork and building an airtight case against Lynda. Braydon had, despite everything, made sure that Nathanial was buried next to his brother. In the end, he'd been the sole attendant at the funeral.

During all of this, Sophia had been discharged from the hospital and had holed up with her sister in Pebblebrook. The detective had seen her twice but they hadn't been alone. Once the paperwork was finished and the case was officially closed, Braydon had decided to throw a surprise party for the beautiful, maddening, stubborn woman because, like Cara had said, she deserved it. Just like the pillows.

"Lisa just called. They're on their way," Richard said, coming in from the back porch. Braydon nodded to the man he'd come to respect and started to usher the party-goers into the living room. It wasn't a big crowd—Cara, Tom, Richard, Jordan, Captain Westin and John the Ticketer—but he hoped she would be pleased. Everyone in attendance may not have known the woman all that well, but there was no denying each person's affection for her.

Minutes later there was a knock on the door and everyone quieted.

"I guess I'll just come right in!" Lisa called, feigning ignorance. She opened the door wide, hurried through and turned to her sister as everyone yelled, "Surprise!"

"Happy birthday!"

Sophia's face instantly turned red, but a smile reached ear to ear. The next half hour was spent talking, drinking and eating. Not once was Nathanial's name mentioned. Braydon watched as the younger Hardwick sister continued to smile. She was the most beautiful woman he'd ever seen.

"Why don't you just ask her to dance already?" Lisa teased, coming out of the kitchen with a slice of cake. "I'm sure she'll say yes."

Braydon laughed, the sound drawing Sophia's attention. She excused herself from the conversation she was having with Cara and walked over.

"I have something for you, by the way," she began, earning an eyebrow raise from the detective. He followed her into the kitchen where she handed him the bag she'd been carrying when she first came in. "It's to say thank-you for everything."

Perplexed, Braydon opened the bag. There was a brand-new pan and spatula inside.

"I noticed that your pan was a little too small for making two grilled cheeses at once," she explained, not stopping for him to question it. "I just figured, since I'll be living in Culpepper now, it might be handy to have."

"Living in Culpepper?" It was the first time they'd talked about her future. Braydon hadn't wanted to have the conversation about Sophia returning to the city. It was one he'd been hoping to avoid.

"I've decided to stay," she said proudly. "Lisa is letting me rent out her house." There was no stopping the smile that attached to Braydon's face.

"What about your job?"

"It wasn't actually as hard to leave it as I thought it would be. Lisa asked me to become a partner in Details and I said yes. I have a better knack for numbers and, I have to admit, it would be fun to be around her again." She paused. "So, I thought if you wanted to—"

Braydon interrupted Sophia by closing the space between them. He kissed her long and hard. It said everything the two of them couldn't form into words. It promised a hopeful future and happiness that Braydon had never felt before. It promised him a life with Sophia.

It promised a life filled with grilled cheese sandwiches.

* * * * *

COMING NEXT MONTH FROM

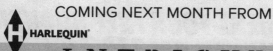

I N T R I G U E

Available April 21, 2015

#1563 SHOWDOWN AT SHADOW JUNCTION
Big "D" Dads: The Daltons • by Joanna Wayne
When Jade Dalton escapes a ruthless kidnapper on the trail of a
multimillion-dollar necklace, Navy SEAL Booker Knox will do whatever
it takes to protect the beautiful event planner. Failure isn't an option.

#1564 TWO SOULS HOLLOW
The Gates • by Paula Graves
Ginny Coltrane might hold the key to proving Anson Daughtry's
innocence. But when Ginny is dragged into a drug war, Anson may be
her only hope of escaping with her life.

#1565 SCENE OF THE CRIME: KILLER COVE
by Carla Cassidy
Accused of murder, Bo McBride has finally returned to Lost Lagoon to
clear his name—with the help of sexy Claire Silver. But as they investigate,
it doesn't take long to realize that danger stalks Claire...

#1566 NAVY SEAL JUSTICE
Covert Cowboys, Inc. • by Elle James
After former Navy SEAL James Monahan and FBI agent Melissa Bradley's
mutual friend goes missing, they join forces to find him. But as a band of
dangerous criminals closes in, survival means trusting each other—their
toughest mission yet.

#1567 COWBOY INCOGNITO
The Brothers of Hastings Ridge Ranch • by Alice Sharpe
A roadtrip to uncover Zane Doe's identity exposes his *real* connection to
Kinsey Frost—and the murderous intentions of those once close to her. Now
Zane must protect her from someone who wants to silence her for good.

#1568 UNDER SUSPICION
Bayou Bonne Chance • by Mallory Kane
Undercover NSA agent Zach Winters vows to solve his best friend's
murder. With the criminals closing in, Zach will risk his own life to protect
a vulnerable widow and her beautiful bodyguard, Madeleine Tierney—the
woman he can't imagine saying goodbye to.

**YOU CAN FIND MORE INFORMATION ON UPCOMING HARLEQUIN® TITLES,
FREE EXCERPTS AND MORE AT WWW.HARLEQUIN.COM.**

HICNM0415

REQUEST YOUR FREE BOOKS!
2 FREE NOVELS PLUS 2 FREE GIFTS!

⊞ HARLEQUIN®

INTRIGUE®

BREATHTAKING ROMANTIC SUSPENSE

YES! Please send me 2 FREE Harlequin Intrigue® novels and my 2 FREE gifts (gifts are worth about $10). After receiving them, if I don't wish to receive any more books, I can return the shipping statement marked "cancel." If I don't cancel, I will receive 6 brand-new novels every month and be billed just $4.74 per book in the U.S. or $5.24 per book in Canada. That's a savings of at least 14% off the cover price! It's quite a bargain! Shipping and handling is just 50¢ per book in the U.S. and 75¢ per book in Canada.* I understand that accepting the 2 free books and gifts places me under no obligation to buy anything. I can always return a shipment and cancel at any time. Even if I never buy another book, the two free books and gifts are mine to keep forever.

182/382 HDN F42N

Name	(PLEASE PRINT)

Address	Apt. #

City	State/Prov.	Zip/Postal Code

Signature (if under 18, a parent or guardian must sign)

Mail to the **Harlequin® Reader Service:**
IN U.S.A.: P.O. Box 1867, Buffalo, NY 14240-1867
IN CANADA: P.O. Box 609, Fort Erie, Ontario L2A 5X3
Are you a subscriber to Harlequin Intrigue books
and want to receive the larger-print edition?
Call 1-800-873-8635 or visit www.ReaderService.com.

* Terms and prices subject to change without notice. Prices do not include applicable taxes. Sales tax applicable in N.Y. Canadian residents will be charged applicable taxes. Offer not valid in Quebec. This offer is limited to one order per household. Not valid for current subscribers to Harlequin Intrigue books. All orders subject to credit approval. Credit or debit balances in a customer's account(s) may be offset by any other outstanding balance owed by or to the customer. Please allow 4 to 6 weeks for delivery. Offer available while quantities last.

Your Privacy—The Harlequin® Reader Service is committed to protecting your privacy. Our Privacy Policy is available online at www.ReaderService.com or upon request from the Harlequin Reader Service.

We make a portion of our mailing list available to reputable third parties that offer products we believe may interest you. If you prefer that we not exchange your name with third parties, or if you wish to clarify or modify your communication preferences, please visit us at www.ReaderService.com/consumerschoice or write to us at Harlequin Reader Service Preference Service, P.O. Box 9062, Buffalo, NY 14269. Include your complete name and address.

HI13R

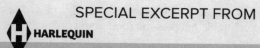
*Bo McBride, accused but never arrested for the murder
of his girlfriend two years ago, has finally returned to
Lost Lagoon, Mississippi, to clear his name with
Claire Silber's help. But it doesn't take long for them
to realize that real danger stalks Claire.*

Read on for a sneak preview of
SCENE OF THE CRIME: KILLER COVE,
the latest crime scene book from
New York Times *bestselling author*
Carla Cassidy.

"So, your turn. Tell me what you've been doing for the last
two years," Claire asked. "Have you made yourself a new,
happy life? Found a new love? I heard through the grapevine
that you're living in Jackson now."

Bo nodded at the same time the sound of rain splattered
against the window. "I opened a little bar and grill, Bo's
Place, although it's nothing like the original." His dark
brows tugged together in a frown, as if remembering the
highly successful business he'd had here in town before he
was ostracized.

He took another big drink and then continued, "There's
no new woman in my life. I don't even have friends. Hell,
I'm not even sure what I'm doing here with you."

"You're here because I'm a bossy woman," she replied.
She got up to refill his glass. "And I thought you could use
an extra friend while you're here."

She handed him the fresh drink and then curled back up

in the corner of the sofa. The rain fell steadily now. She turned on the end table lamp as the room darkened with the storm.

For a few minutes they remained silent. She could tell by his distant stare toward the opposite wall that he was lost inside his head.

Despite his somber expression, she couldn't help but feel a physical attraction to him that she'd never felt before. Still, that wasn't what had driven her to seek contact with him, to invite him into her home. She had an ulterior motive.

A low rumble of thunder seemed to pull him out of his head. He focused on her and offered a small smile of apology. "Sorry about that. I got lost in thoughts of everything I need to get done before I leave town."

"I wanted to talk to you about that," she said.

He raised a dark brow. "About all the things I need to take care of?"

"No, about you leaving town."

"What about it?"

She drew a deep breath, knowing she was putting her nose in business that wasn't her own, and yet unable to stop herself. "Doesn't it bother you knowing that Shelly's murderer is still walking these streets, free as a bird?"

His eyes narrowed slightly. "Why are you so sure I'm innocent?" he asked.

Don't miss
SCENE OF THE CRIME: KILLER COVE
by New York Times *bestselling author Carla Cassidy,*
available May 2015 wherever
Harlequin® Intrigue books and ebooks are sold.

www.Harlequin.com

Love the Harlequin book you just read?

Your opinion matters.

Review this book on your favorite book site, review site, blog or your own social media properties and share your opinion with other readers!

THE WORLD IS BETTER WITH

Romance

Harlequin has everything from contemporary, passionate and heartwarming to suspenseful and inspirational stories.

Whatever your mood, we have a romance just for you!

Connect with us to find your next great read, special offers and more.

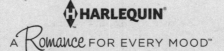

Ⓗ HARLEQUIN®

A *Romance* FOR EVERY MOOD™